My China Story

New Adventures

第三只眼看中国

我与中国共成长

王新玲 杨丹 主编

U0820082

SinolinguA
华语教学出版社

First Edition 2021
Third Printing 2023

ISBN 978-7-5138-2082-0
Copyright 2021 by Sinolingua Co., Ltd
Published by Sinolingua Co., Ltd
24 Baiwanzhuang Street, Beijing 100037, China
Tel: (86)10-68320585, 68997826
Fax: (86)10-68997826, 68326333
http://www.sinolingua.com.cn
E-mail: hyjx@sinolingua.com.cn
Printed by Beijing Hucais Culture Communication Co., Ltd.

Printed in the People's Republic of China

编委会

总策划

黄玉龙　王君校

策　划

戴　凡

主　编

王新玲　杨　丹

本册图书中的视频由中国外文局煦方国际传媒及中国网提供

主创人员

钟　磊　栗盼盼　任柏鑫　李帝璇　张若梦　郜玉至　韩歆昊

房小棋　李凯馨

PREFACE

In recent years, platforms and services featuring short videos are trending across the globe. More and more international friends pick up their mobile phones and video cameras to record their lives, travels, and work experience in China. They have become narrators of their own Chinese stories and ambassadors of friendly exchanges between China and other countries. Some are engaged in international trade, especially key projects associated with the "Belt and Road Initiative", contributing their wisdom to international economic cooperation. Some have ventured to the rural areas and are helping farmers out of poverty; some work in the sports industry in China, creating new glories in their games; some are dedicated to research in science and the humanities; and some are engaged in the media. Though they come from different countries, they are making great contributions everywhere in China.

Through their lenses, these foreign friends present their unique perspectives of China, telling stories of the country's development, of shaking off poverty and achieving moderate prosperity, of creating new hopes despite adversities, and of interactions with the rest of the world. These stories show their understanding and care for contemporary China, its people, and the changes taking place in the country, explaining their thoughts on China's reform and development, and showing the growing optimism of the Chinese people.

The "My China Story" book series is based on the prize-winning works of the Global Short Video Contest of the same name and features rich images with intriguing stories that are representative of Chinese culture and entertaining to overseas readers. But even more interesting is seeing how people from all over the world who have discovered a new purpose in China are not so different from those of ordinary Chinese people. The books show us that we all share the same desire to pursue our dreams, no matter where we come from.

The books recount the rich, diverse experiences of short video creators in China as they try local Chinese food, visit scenic and historic spots, witness local residents' lives, and enjoy the conveniences brought about by smart technologies. But it also shows a deeper view, offering first-hand experiences of personal contacts between the East and West, tradition and modernity, and the cultural collisions that sometimes occur. Living their lives as the locals, these authors present the rapid development taking place in the country's urban and rural regions, as well as in various trades and professions. They have deep relationships with their Chinese counterparts and use their cameras to reflect the optimism, generosity, and kindness of equally ordinary Chinese from all walks of life.

Each author has faithfully recorded his or her own story, giving readers a true profile of China through an authentic and objective account. To learn more about a country, the best way is to come and see it for yourself and to walk the streets in person. After working and living here for a period of time as these video creators have, perhaps you, too, will find something fascinating in this mysterious, ancient, and yet modern country.

前言

近两年来，短视频平台在全世界范围内火热兴起，越来越多的外国友人拿起手机和摄像机记录在中国的日常见闻、旅行趣事、工作心得，成为了中国故事的讲述者、中外友好交流的践行者：他们有的活跃在中外贸易领域，尤其是“一带一路”沿线重点工程，为中外经济合作付出智慧；有的扎根农村，为中国农村脱贫致富贡献力量；有的化身体育大使，在中国的赛场上重铸辉煌；有的从事科技和人文研究；有的从事媒体行业；有的从事文学创作……他们来自不同国家，活跃在中国的各个行业。

这些外国人通过手中的镜头展现出看中国的独特视角和新奇视点，讲述了他们眼中的中国发展、脱贫奔小康、在艰难中创造生活的希望，以及与世界交往的时代故事，表达了他们心中对当代中国人与中国事的认知和看法，诠释了世界各国人民对中国改革发展和中国人民乐观向上心态的理解和思考。

“第三只眼看中国”系列丛书基于“第三只眼看中国”全球短视频大赛获奖作品编写而成，故事性强，图片丰富，具有极高的可读性和趣味性。丛书汇聚了全球短视频创作者的力量，把海外受众关注的，能够代表中国文化特色的，能够体现中国与世界共同、共通之处的故事传播出去，对于推动人文交流、增进民心相通、促进文化传播具有重要意义。

本书记录了短视频创作者们在中国多姿多彩、妙趣横生的生活，他们除了品尝美食，游览名胜，感受民生，体验智能生活带来的诸多便利，更亲身体会到了东方和西方、传统与现代之间的文化碰撞。创作者们化身为普通老百姓在中国生活，专注于在中国发展自己的事业。他们扎根于中国，通过自己的故事来反映20多年来中国的城市农村、各行各业的快速发展；他们与普通中国人建立起深厚的友谊，通过镜头勾勒出中国老百姓乐观、豁达、和善的民族性格和气质形象。

本书的每位作者都忠实记录了自己在中国的故事，客观、真实地为外国读者提供了一个又一个了解中国的侧面。如果你想了解更立体、更直观的中国，最好的方式就是亲自来中国看一看、走一走，工作和生活上一段时间，也许你从此就会爱上这个神秘的国度。

目录 | CONTENTS

夏爱克在中国大山里的 16 年

Eckehard Scharfschwerdt's Years in China's Mountainous Region

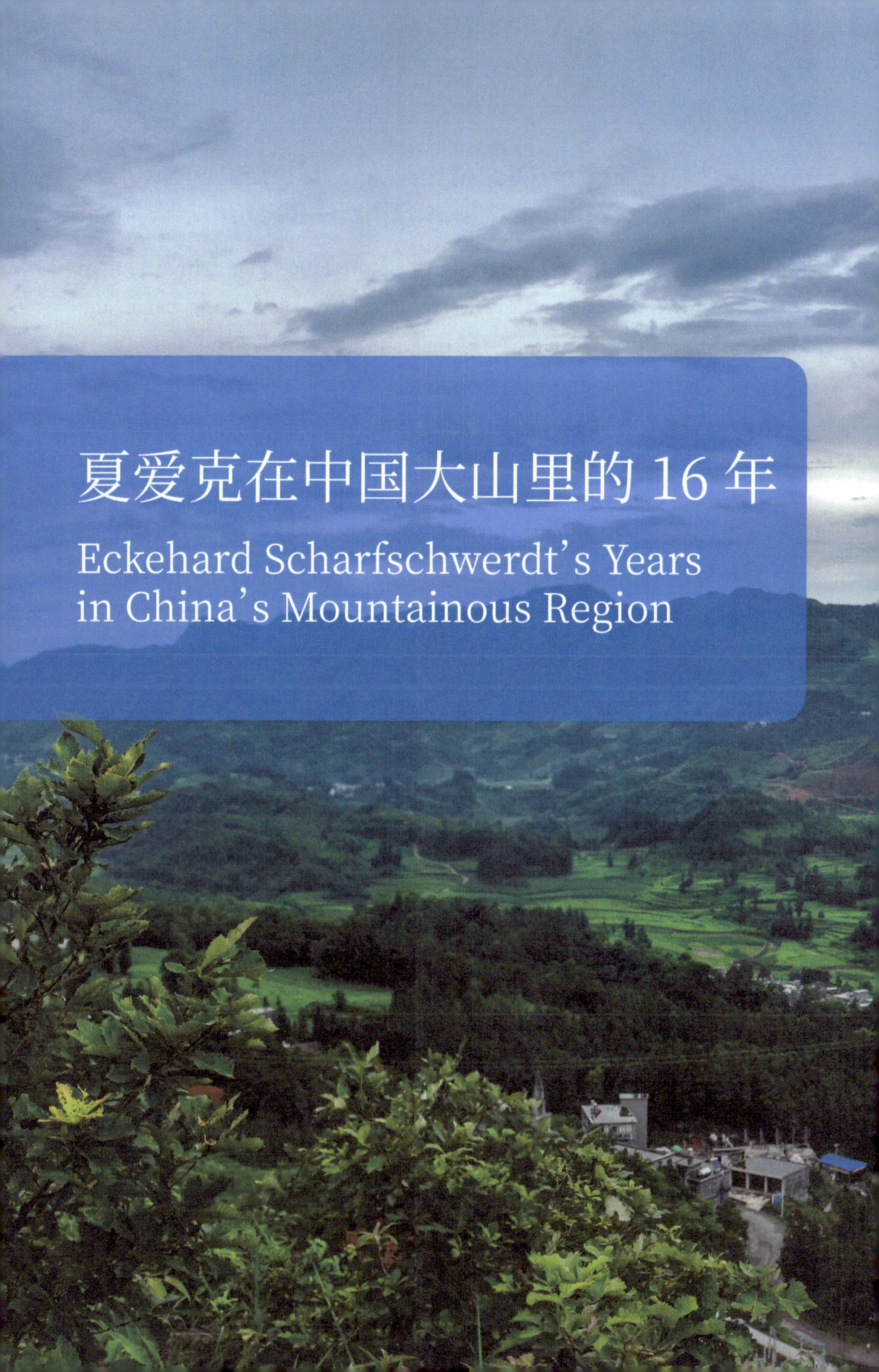

Eckehard Scharfschwerdt's Years in China's Mountainous Region

Heqing County is located south of the Hengduan Mountains in northwestern Yunnan Province, southwest China, and it is remote and unknown to most Chinese people. On a sunny day in August 2019, a tall, thin foreign man with gray hair arrived at the county hospital, wearing a green checkered shirt and carrying a blue backpack. He spoke Chinese fluently and happily shook hands with doctors who greeted him with a broad smile, saying, "It's so nice to see you again many years later." The foreign man is the German doctor named Eckehard Scharfschwerdt. He is called China's "modern Norman Bethune". (Norman Bethune, a Canadian surgeon who came to Yan'an in 1938 to help Chinese people during their war against Japanese aggression).

Eckehard was born in a small town in the southwestern German state of Baden-Württemberg in the 1960s. After graduating from the

Department of Medicine at Göttingen University, he participated in medical aid programs in Indonesia and Nepal. In 2000, Eckehard and his wife began volunteering medical aid at county hospitals in Heqing, Jianshui and Honghe in Yunan Province, and cemented ties with the people from the mountainous region. For 16 years, he has provided medical services and aid to the people living there and witnessed the development of China's impoverished region. In 2017, he was granted the "Friendship Award" by the Chinese government and delivered a speech as a representative of 50 award winners. The "Friendship Award" is the highest honor given by the Chinese government to foreign experts who make outstanding contributions to China's modernization. From 1991 to 2017, the award had been conferred on 1,549 foreign experts from 70 countries.

Speaking of his story of having lived for 16 years in China, Eckehard often uses the phrase "purpose of life" to describe the reason for his coming to China. In the late 1990s, he was a doctor in training. He and his wife joined a non-profit organization responsible for sending volunteers to East Asia. At that time, China needed doctors. They knew nothing about China and were worried about their work and life there, but something happened which dispelled their misgivings. While on duty in an ambulance one day, Eckehard saved a drowning girl. The girl woke up two days later and expressed her gratitude to them. Eckehard discovered that she was Chinese. Her gratitude made him feel that he was not unfamiliar with China. That was how Eckehard decided to come to China to help more people.

In August 2000, Eckechard came to Kunming City, Yunnan Province with some volunteers to study Chinese. In 2001, he began working in Heqing County People's Hospital as a consultant. He still remembers what the hospital looked like when he arrived there for the first time. It was quite small and simple, with only a little medical equipment. It had only an electrocardiograph and an ultrasonic diagnostic apparatus. He assisted in general anesthesia and operation. He helped purchase medical supplies for the hospital, and train medical staff. He would also travel long distances to provide medical treatment to people in the mountainous areas. In these remote areas, villagers were apprehensive and even afraid to meet a foreigner for the first time. Eckehard and the volunteers did a lot to win their trust and acceptance. Over the past 16 years, he has traveled from Heqing to Jianshui and Honghe, and has

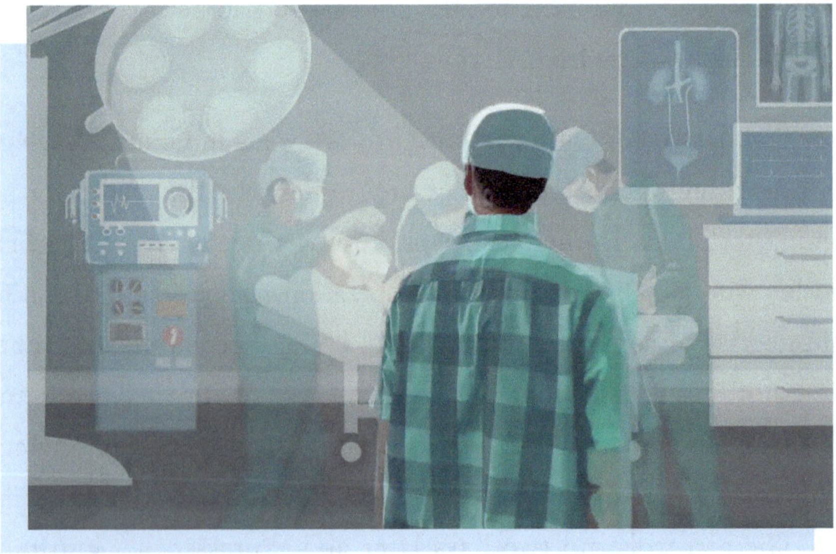

contributed significantly to the improvement of local medical services. He says that it has been very difficult and he has even encountered some cultural misunderstandings. However, he says that he is still inspired. "At that time, the medical apparatus and medicine in the hospitals were limited, and medical conditions were not good. But the doctors are willing to learn, and this is very important." As the medical staff are willing to learn and exchange their medical experience, this further strengthens his willingness to provide medical aid.

During his trips to the villages, Eckehard also taught English in local schools and even helped with some poverty alleviation work. Because of their frequent contacts, Eckehard and the local villagers became more familiar with one another. Villagers knew that the non-profit organization in which he worked raised sheep in Sichuan Province, so they asked if he could help them raise goats where they lived. Eckehard then came up with the idea of lending five goats to each family who would give back five goats after three years. He rode bikes from village to village, asking who raised goats and who wanted to sell their goats. He also took some red paint along. If he found a goat he wanted to buy and its price was agreed upon, he painted its head red. Eckehard was also able to give some medical consultation to the villagers who needed help with their goats. He says that he felt the true meaning of the phrase, "helping others help themselves", and has got friendship and respect there, and has even been invited to local wedding ceremonies or temple sacrificial rituals. Eckehard and other volunteers are treated as family members. In his poverty alleviation work, he has known the wisdom of the villagers. He stayed in the home of his friend Nongfa while helping the villagers build a water pool. In the process of building it, Nongfa, who received only two- to

three-year primary school education, came up with a better idea. With his eyes glistening, Eckehard says excitedly, "Nongfa loves to build something creatively and he has good ideas about how we could do it better."

Eckehard has witnessed the great changes that have taken place in China over the past 16 years. On his trip back to Heqing County in 2019, he saw that the county hospital has become larger, and the muddy paths in mountainous areas have been wide, smooth cement roads. What he is most excited about and admires, however, is the introduction of a new rural cooperative health system for the farmers. It is a new healthcare insurance program for China's huge rural population, launched by the Chinese government in 2002. Farmers are encouraged to join the program which is funded by individuals, the collective, and the government. As the program provides basic medical insurance for poor villagers, Eckehard is very excited about it. "I remember that the local government implemented the program in 2006. The local government increases the subsidy every year, and more and more farmers are joining the program. So they pay 10 RMB yuan each, and the local government 40 RMB yuan, and they have basic health insurance the next year." It is the medical care insurance program that enables farmers' access to better medical services. Eckehard admires the Chinese government's continued financial support in the rural medical and health care.

Eckehard has countless stories of his 16-year life in China. It is here that he knows about China for the first time and that he has spent his youth in the mountainous region providing medical aid to the people of Yunnan who have accepted and welcomed him. Seeing them become independent and innovative, Eckehard has acquired a deeper understanding of life. "I think that without faith I wouldn't have come here, because it meant giving up a lot in the beginning. At that time, we thought that maybe we could stay for ten years as long as we put in effort and made this worthwhile. But after getting used to living there, I loved the villagers all the more so that I didn't want to leave. I feel that I am half Chinese." Pursuing a goal in his life is the reason for his coming to China, and he has found the meaning of life in the mountainous region.

夏爱克在中国大山里的 16 年

这里是中国西南地区云南省的鹤庆县。鹤庆县位于云南省的西北部，滇西横断山脉的南端，是一个对大部分中国人而言都较为陌生、偏远的县城。2019 年 8 月，阳光正好，在这个偏远县城的县医院里，一个穿着绿色格子衬衫，背着蓝色双肩包，身材瘦瘦高高，头发花白、鼻梁高挺的外国人说着一口流利的中国话，开心地和医生们握手。随着不断地握手和“你好，你好”的响起，医生们笑容满面地说着：“很高兴，这么多年，又一次见到你。”一个“又一次”道尽了久别重逢的欢喜和对这个外国人的欢迎。这个来到

中国大山里的外国人就是德国医生夏爱克，他被中国人称为“当代白求恩”。

夏爱克出生于 20 世纪 60 年代德国巴符州的一个小镇上。他在哥廷根大学医学专业毕业后，曾参加过在印尼和尼泊尔的医疗援助项目。2000 年，夏爱克和妻子一起来到中国的云南，来到鹤庆、建水、红河等县城医院进行志愿医疗援助，也和大山里的人们结下了深厚的友谊。夏爱克为这里的人们提供了 16 年的医疗服务和援助，也见证了这 16 年间中国贫困地区的发展。2017 年，夏爱克被中国政府授予了“友谊奖”并代表当年 50 名获奖者在颁奖大会上发言。“友谊奖”是中国政府为表彰在中国现代化建设中做出突出贡献的外国专家设立的最高荣誉奖项。自 1991 年至 2017 年，共有来自 70 个国家的 1549 名外国专家获奖。

说起和中国 16 年的故事，夏爱克用“寻找人生”这样一个充满了信仰和理想的词来描述来到中国的缘由。在 20 世纪 90 年代末，夏爱克还是一个德国的见习医生。为了寻找人生的目标，他和妻子一起加入了一个公益

组织。这个公益组织将各种工作人员输送到东亚地区。当时，只有中国需要医生。那时的夏爱克和妻子都对中国一无所知，也对去中国生活和工作充满了顾虑。但后来的一件事改变了他们的焦虑不安。夏爱克在德国救护车当班时救了一个溺水的女孩。两天后女孩醒来，激动地向他们道谢。夏爱克发现这是一个中国女孩，而这个中国女孩的道谢让他感到中国好像也没那么陌生。于是，夏爱克最后下定决心去中国帮助更多的人。

2000年8月，夏爱克和志愿者们一起到达云南昆明学习中文。2001年，夏爱克作为顾问加入了鹤庆县人民医院。夏爱克还清晰地记得，第一次来的时候，鹤庆县人民医院还是一个“小小的小医院”，什么都很简单，医院的设备很少，整个医院只有一台心电图和一台B超机。夏爱克既在手术室里帮忙做全身麻醉，又帮助医院购买一些小的医疗物资，还负责对医院的工作人员进行医疗培训。在这些工作之外，夏爱克还会跋山涉水去为大山深处的农村老百姓诊疗。说起下乡为村民诊疗，夏爱克说，这些地方非常的偏僻，村民们第一次见到外国人都会感到恐惧和担心。夏爱克和自己的同伴下了很大的工夫才获得村民们的信任，被村民们接受。从鹤庆到建水再到红河，16年间，夏爱克辗转数地，在大山里的乡村与小镇之间为当地的医疗服务水平提升做出了自己的贡献。辛苦吗？当然很辛苦，也会遭遇许多文化的隔膜。但是夏爱克却很振奋地提到："那时医院的器械和药物都很有限，条件也不好，但是医生们都很愿意学习，这让我觉得我的工作很重要。"正是这些大山深处的医疗工作者们积极好学、乐于交流的态度让夏爱克提供医疗援助的意愿更加坚定。

在下乡诊疗的过程中，夏爱克也在乡下的学校进行英文教学，甚至还做起了扶贫工作。说起自己的扶贫工作，夏爱克清晰地记得是当地农民们主动提出的需求。因为他长期下乡和村民们熟悉了，有一次，一些村民就提出“你们组织有在四川养羊的经验，能否在这儿帮村民养羊？”夏爱克和他的伙伴们了解到了村民的需求后，想出了“借羊养羊”的项目计划。也就是说，他们借给每个家庭五只山羊，三年后这些家庭再归还五只山羊。为了让这个计划能够顺利开展，夏爱克经常骑着自行车穿行在大山之间，每到一个村子就问“谁在养羊？谁要卖羊？”他还随身带着红色的颜料，一旦谈妥了要买的山羊和价格就在山羊的头顶上做好红色标记。他不辞辛劳，从不抱怨。同时，在帮助村民养羊的过程中，夏爱克曾跟随一个养羊的家庭在山里放羊，了解了许多牲畜的患病情况，为村民提供关于羊群的医疗咨询。在这里，夏爱克感受到了“助人者自助”的意义，也在这片大山里收获了友谊和尊重。不少村民会在举行婚礼或者寺庙祭祀活动时邀请夏爱克和他的同伴们参加，像对待家人一样对待他们。夏爱克还在扶贫工作中了解了

村民们的智慧。夏爱克在村里的时候常常住在自己的好友农发（音）家里。最初，夏爱克帮助农发等家庭修建蓄水池。在修建蓄水池的过程中，只接受过两三年小学教育的农发根据当地情况想出了更好的主意。提到自己这位挚友时，夏爱克眼里闪着光，兴奋地说：“农发在工程建造上富有创造性。他确实喜欢建造，而且有好的想法，还可以做到更好。”夏爱克的友善、奉献与无私和农发的接纳、互助与智慧结合，成就了一段感人的友谊。

夏爱克在云南大山里服务、奉献的 16 年也是他见证中国发展的 16 年。他认为，中国的发展变化实在是太大了。2019 年重返鹤庆的旅程中，他看到了鹤庆县医院从小到大的变化，看到了山里的道路从泥泞颠簸的小道变成宽阔平坦的水泥路的变化。而在中国所有的发展变化中，最令夏爱克兴奋又佩服的是在农村医疗中推行“新农合”政策。“新农合”政策是中国政府在2002年提出的引导农民建立以大病统筹为主的新型农村合作医疗制度。在这个制度之下，政府组织、引导和支持农民自愿参加，通过个人、集体和政府多方筹资，采取个人缴纳一定费用、集体扶持贫困家庭和政府补贴资助大部分费用的方式来为农民提供医疗资助。说起这个政策，夏爱克非常激动，他认为这为底层的农民，尤其是那些贫困的农民建立了基本的医疗保障。他回忆道：“如果没有记错的话，

我记得当地的政府是在2006年推行的。最开始，政府试推了几年，

每年都增加补贴。后来自愿加入的农民就越来越多。他们自己只用出 10 元钱，然后政府出 40 元钱，这些村民们就能享受到下一年的基础医疗保障。”正是这些医疗保障制度让更多的村民享受到了更好的医疗服务。夏爱克非常钦佩中国政府能在医疗健康领域持续投入这么多。

说起在中国的这 16 年，夏爱克有数不清的故事和说不完的情感。在这里，他第一次认识了中国，也把自己的青春奉献在了大山之中。他为云南地区的人们提供了及时的医疗服务，帮助了许许多多贫困的人们；与此同时，他也被这些人所接纳、欢迎，也在这些人的自立、自助和智慧中获得生命的感悟和人生的厚度。夏爱克深情地说：“如果没有信念，我最开始就不会来这里，因为这意味着要放弃很多。我们当时说可以在这里住十年，多付出努力，让这件事更有价值。但真正适应这里的生活后，我越来越喜欢这里的人们，我感觉真的离不开了。我是半个中国人。”寻找人生的目标是夏爱克来中国的缘由，他在中国的大山里找到了他人生的意义。

Scan for a Video

美国哥儿俩在中国当农民

Two American Men's Story of Becoming Farmers in China

Two American Men's Story of Becoming Farmers in China

Here on the vast Qinghai-Tibet Plateau, villages are scattered across the farmland which stretches for as far as the eye could see. In a rural village in northwest China's Qinghai Province, large greenhouses stand out conspicuously. They are an organic vegetable farm set up by two American men. Approaching you, they seem like tourists, even like computer programmers from Silicon Valley, until you notice the accumulated mud on their shoes. They are Daniel Willers and Morgan Jones, two American men who are farming in China.

Daniel is tall with a blonde beard. He wears a gray checkered shirt, light-color jeans, and metal-brimmed glasses. He left the US in 2013, and he has been in China for six and a half years. Morgan is a half head shorter than Daniel and wears an orange checkered shirt and dark blue jeans. He is from California, and he arrived earlier than Daniel. He has been in China for over ten years. When he first came to Qinghai, he wanted to work in agriculture.

They grow over 30 kinds of vegetables and fruit, such as eggplant, cabbage, collard greens, celery, bok choy and strawberry. Since 2000, there has been a growing demand for agricultural products with higher quality and health safety standards in China. Morgan and Daniel's initial plan was simply to grow their food according to international food safety standards, but Chinese consumers thought that this meant the food was "organic," which was not technically correct. They decided to change their cultivation methods to meet this market demand and set a new development direction — to go completely organic.

Using organic methods sets higher requirements on the environment, the planting process and even the land itself. To protect the environment and maintain sustainable development of the Qinghai-Tibet Plateau and its soil fertility, Morgan and Daniel learned from local farmers how to replenish the land by using organic fertilizer. They obtain a variety of compost ingredients from local villagers like seed rape, potatoes and other agricultural waste, mix them together, add water, wait until the temperature rises to 55°C and turn them at least three times. This produces organic compost which is pollution-free. While showing us their compost, Daniel grasps a handful of the organic fertilizer, and smells it as if it were treasure.

The farm's success is attributed not only to the large consumer market and high-quality organic fertilizer, but also to the convenient logistical system and the internet. "We pick the vegetables in the morning, package them around the midday and deliver them in the afternoon." Because of the advanced logistical system in China, the fresh vegetables can be quickly delivered to remote villages like those on the Qinghai-Tibet Plateau. This makes it possible for Morgan and Daniel to provide safe, healthy, and fresh agricultural products at a more competitive price in China's market. They mainly rely on their online shop accessed through WeChat to exhibit and sell their products. Customers can find their favorite products in the e-shop, place orders and pay online. Also, they try to avoid using pesticides to ensure their vegetables are safe and healthy. In the event of a pest outbreak, they will use natural physical and biological remedies. For example, they use ladybugs to eliminate aphids on eggplants, which they bought on Taobao.com, the well-known e-shop platform most Chinese use.

Morgan and Daniel have integrated Chinese and American agriculture practices into their farming. For example, they use local methods of creating compost to fertilize the land, but adopt a practice popular in the US that informs customers about the place of origin and

the producer. The good name of the producer guarantees that their products are safe and fresh. Each package is labeled with the name of the farm and also the producer. This combination of Chinese and American farming methods is becoming quite popular with the farmers and customers.

Morgan and Daniel also try to cooperate with local farmers, and this in turn helps them expand their own business, thus achieving win-win results. Apart from vegetables, they sell Qinghai specialties like Qinghai honey. The honey, which is supplied by local partners, is collected from the rape seed along the Qinghai Lake. Morgan and Daniel are also using the local marketing channels they've opened up to promote other local specialty products grown by other farmers. In earlier years, incomes from agriculture in remote rural areas like Qinghai were very low, and many Qinghai farmers left the farms and migrated to the cities to earn a living. But in recent years, thanks to the government's poverty alleviation efforts, Morgan and Daniel began to encourage local farmers to focus on growing specialty products, like quinoa. Daniel gently touches the quinoa seedlings and says emotionally, "The quinoa grows well with the dry climate, high altitude and soils that aren't super-fertile on the Qinghai-Tibet Plateau. We work together with the government to help farmers grow quinoa and sell it." This is conducive to developing eco-friendly and sustainable agriculture and making the local farmers improve their living standards. Agriculture is crucial to human survival. Morgan and Daniel have put their roots down in this remote rural area of China. They are living proof that those who are close to agriculture and the soil will eventually be rewarded by the land.

美国哥儿俩在中国当农民

在辽阔的、天空低垂的青藏高原上，村落疏疏散布，广袤的农田延伸到无尽的远方。在中国西北部青海省的一个农村，一大片大棚格外显眼。这片大棚是两个美国小伙儿在这里的蔬菜基地。当这两个美国小伙儿走过来的时候，如果不刻意观察他们脚上新旧沉积的泥土，我们会以为他俩是两个来旅游的游客，尤其像硅谷地区的程序员。他俩就是在中国当农民种地的美国小伙子Daniel Willers和Morgan Jones。

Daniel高高壮壮，留着金色络腮胡，戴着文雅的金属框眼镜，灰白色格子衬衫搭着浅色牛仔裤。他2013年从美国来到中国，

已经在中国待了8年了。Morgan比Daniel矮半头，也穿着格子衬衫和牛仔裤，不过他的衬衫是橘色格子，牛仔裤是深蓝色。当他说话的时候，他的右眉会不自觉地往上挑。Morgan来自美国的加利福利亚，比Daniel更早来中国，他已经在青海待了十多年。他初来中国青海的时候，就想在这里从事农业有关的工作。

这哥儿俩的大棚里种着茄子、圆白菜、羽衣甘蓝、芹菜、上海青、草莓等30多种蔬菜和水果，一片欣欣向荣的样子。而这些蔬菜水果全都是按照国际标准种植出来的健康安全的蔬菜。2000年之后，中国经济的飞速发展让越来越多的消费者对农业产品的安全健康提出了更高的要求，这就为他们如此深耕细作的产品销售提供了广阔的市场。最开始顾客们都认为他们卖的是有机蔬菜，这让他们对自己的农业种植提出了新的发展方向——种植有机蔬菜。

有机蔬菜的种植对环境和种植过程乃至土地都提出了更高的要求。为了保护环境，实现青藏高原地区土地的可持续发展，保持土地的肥力，Morgan和Daniel从中国农民那里学到了“沤肥”这种给土地补充有机肥料的方法。他们从村民那儿找到各种堆肥的原料，比如油菜、土豆和其他农作物废料，把这些全部混在一起，然后加水，等温度上升到55度，再至少翻三次。这样可以自然形成有机肥料，绿色无污染。介绍到他们的绿色肥料时，Daniel抓起一把正在沤肥过程中的有机肥料，左右倒腾，捧起来闻一闻，如同宝贝一般珍视。

在中国当农民、种植有机蔬菜，不仅仅是消费市场和有机肥料让Morgan和Daniel的农业事业发展壮大，更重要的是这里还有便捷的物流运输和网络销售的渠道。Morgan和Daniel一边将蔬菜从土里拔出来、清理干净、装袋，一边介绍：“早上采摘蔬菜，中午包装，下午就可以将新鲜的蔬菜发往各地。”正是中国现代发达的物流业，让即使偏远如青藏高原的农村也能实现新鲜蔬菜的及时运输。这就为Morgan和Daniel打造安全、健康、新鲜的农产品提供了条件，也让他们的农产品在广大的中国市场上有了更强的竞争力。他们的蔬菜水果主要依靠在社交平台微信上开设的微店实现展示和销售。远在千里之外的顾客可以在微店上查看产品并下单，然后通过微信支付，便捷顺畅。说起这些农产品种植和销售的便利条件时，Morgan 还提到了中国人最喜欢用的“万能”淘宝。为了让蔬菜生长健康、安全，他们不会用很多杀虫剂。一旦爆发虫害，他们会尽量采用生物和物理控制法来对付，例如用七星瓢虫来对付茄子上的蚜虫。而这些七星瓢虫则是从淘宝上大量购买的，非常方便。说到这里的时候，Morgan 笑了，显得轻松愉快。

对 Morgan 和 Daniel 来说，在中国当农民种植农产品，他们会不自觉地学习和融合中美两种不同的农业文化的方式。例如：

在种植的过程中采用非常当地化的沤肥的方法做有机肥料；而在网络销

售的过程中，他们则采用美国农业“责任制”的方式，让顾客知道蔬菜来自哪里，是谁种的，以个人的信誉来保障食品的安全和新鲜。在他们销售的每一份蔬菜和水果的包装上都标明了所在地农场与责任人的名字。这种中美农业种植文化方式的合流似乎也很受他们及消费者的欢迎。

Morgan和Daniel认为，他们在中国青海当农民的另一个意义在于和当地的村民合作共赢，或者说他们也是在帮助当地的村民。他们的事业发展得不错，扩大经营的同时他们也不忘带动周边的农户，把自身的发展变成合作共赢的发展。他们在主营蔬菜的同时也会卖一些青海的特产，比如青海蜂蜜。这些蜂蜜是从青海湖边的油菜花田采集来的，由当地的合作伙伴向他们供应。同时，Morgan和Daniel还利用自己已经打开的农业销售渠道帮忙推广青海的特产，希望当地的农民能够通过特产种植提高收入，留在本地。青海广大偏远地区的农村和中国大部分偏远地区的农村一样，早些年由于农业种植经济收入低，农民们纷纷抛弃土地进城打工谋生。近几年，在中国政府的扶贫政策支持下，Morgan和Daniel开始带动周边农民种植藜麦，希望能够给当地农民带来更多的经济收入，把农民留下来，改善农民的生活。Daniel轻轻抚摸着他们种下的藜麦苗，充满温情地说："青藏高原气候干旱，海拔高，土地相对贫瘠，但是很适合藜麦的生长。我们不仅需要和政府一起带动大家去种植，还需要帮助当地的农民打开藜麦的销售市场。"他们是在做有意义的事情，不仅仅是发展生态可持续的安全、健康农业，也是在帮助当地人通过农业发展改善生活。在全世界，农业都是人类赖以生存的基础。Morgan和Daniel在中国这片遥远的热土扎根，做亲近农业、亲近土地的人，终将会被土地给予丰厚的回报。

Scan for a Video

荷兰夫妇的中国创业史

A Dutch Couple's Story of Doing Business in China

A Dutch Couple's Story of Doing Business in China

I first met the Steendam couple in their shop AmdoCraft in Xining City, Qinghai Province on the Qinghai-Tibet Plateau. They mainly sell woven handicrafts made by Tibetan herdsmen. These handicrafts including hats, bags and ropes show Tibetan culture and customs and hang on the exhibition stands and walls. Of these, bags are of various designs and all sizes, and include wallets, backpacks and cloth bags. The shop is frequented by both Chinese and foreigners, and is popular with the local Tibetan people. The Dutch couple wear blush on their faces, just like the local Tibetan people. This shows that they have lived here for a long time.

Klaas Steendam and his wife Pia de Vries are from the Netherlands. They came to Qinghai in 1998 and have stayed for over 20 years. Their two sons have grown up in Qinghai, so their family could be considered as natives of Qinghai.

Unlike many foreigners who want to live in China to explore its mysteries, Klaas and Pia came just to help those in need. Qinghai Province is an underdeveloped region in China, so few foreigners wanted to live here over 20 years ago. At that time, Klaas was young, and was learning business and marketing in the Netherlands. His family also did business, and his parents had hoped that he would take over their family business. But he did not want to live a life like his father who had spent all his time and energy on making money. After he met Pia, who had graduated with a major in social development studies, he found that she wanted to go abroad to help those in need around the world. Klaas believed that he could work with Pia and use his business expertise to help others. This is how they came to Qinghai together.

Pia says that they didn't expect that they would start this kind of business, but something happened, which inspired them. When they arrived in Qinghai in 1998, the couple was trying different business ventures while learning Chinese. One day, a Tibetan college student came to their home. Having heard that a foreign couple was here and wanted to help the local villagers, he invited them to visit his village. After ten-hour bus ride from Xining, they had to take a tractor to his village in a remote area of the valley. The whole journey was long and arduous. The couple found that the village was isolated and poor with no infrastructure such as schools and roads, but it did produce an abundant amount of wool and yak hair. If these two products were sold to middlemen, the villagers wouldn't make any money. "But the handicrafts they wove with the wool and yak hair have typical Tibetan characteristics and are very attractive," says Pia. "We can see they are very adept at choosing good wool for weaving and knitting." The couple decided to help the villagers weave these handicrafts.

At first, they planned to provide some technical training to the villagers and let them sell their handicrafts themselves. But after a while they discovered that the villagers only needed to be familiar with modern work flows in terms of technical training as they were very creative and showed superb weaving skills. Their biggest problem was marketing. Most of the villagers had never even been to a city, so they did not know how to sell their handicrafts. The couple, therefore, focused on exploring marketing channels and customers. They established the Tibetan Handicrafts Company. Later, they expanded their business from this village to other villages. They have established stable partnerships with four villages to help the villagers increase their incomes.

In Tibetan culture, men often sew and make clothing. Pia began to encourage the women to select the wool and weave the handicrafts. In this way, more people can be involved in the production process, and it is very important for the women in this underdeveloped region to get incomes. This was a wise decision. The couple initially thought that customers would buy the handicrafts woven by women to help lift women out of poverty, but they soon saw the beauty of these handicrafts. Customers not only wanted to support the women, but were also attracted to their beautiful handicrafts. Actually, many non-profit enterprises in China support women in underdeveloped regions. Their development can be attributed not only to customers who support their cause, but also to the customers' true love of the handicrafts designed and woven by these women.

In the beginning, only foreign tourists who visited their shop in Xining bought their handicrafts. As the couple and the villagers collaborated on designing and weaving more beautiful and useful handicrafts, a growing number of Chinese tourists also bought them. Nowadays, most of the customers in the shop are from Beijing, Shanghai and other big Chinese cities. But the couple is especially proud that even local Tibetan people will also buy their handicrafts. Pia showed us a

handicraft in the shop, which is popular among local Tibetan people and all tourists. The handicraft is a long bag shaped like a bucket with blue embroidered Tibetan-style patterns. People often carry it across their backs in a slanted way. This handicraft was designed by a herdsman who has been cooperating with the couple for a long time. As long as the villagers have opportunities, they can show their brilliant ingenuity and craftsmanship.

Although at first their business did not proceed smoothly and they led a hard life, the couple feels no regret. Klaas recalls his hard life in a small village over 20 years ago. There was no bathroom and running water in his house. If they wanted to wash their faces on a winter morning, they would have to spend a lot of time first melting the ice and then heating it. "Life was hard at that time," he says. But they found a new meaning of life after they left the Netherlands, the lowest country in the world, and came to Qinghai, the place with an average altitude of over 3,000 meters above the sea level. Here, they have not only helped local villagers, but they have also succeeded in business. They say that life in China is very different from that in the Netherlands, which is also meaningful. Doing business in China not only marks a new starting point in the couple's life, but also helps them attain goals in their life.

荷兰夫妇的中国创业史

第一次见到Klaas夫妇，是在他们经营的自主品牌Klaas Steendam的店里。这家店位于中国青藏高原上的青海省西宁市，主要卖一些藏族牧民的手工艺品。店里的展柜和墙上都摆满了极具藏族风情的各种编织品，主要是帽子、包包、绳带等。其中品类、花样最多的就是各色包包，例如巴掌大小的钱包、斜着背的羊毛背包、单挎的布袋方包。总是有客人在店里参观或者选购物品，外国人、中国人都有，甚至还有一些穿着传统藏族服饰的中国人。看起来这家店开得很

成功，也很受本地人的欢迎。而 Klaas 夫妇脸上和当地藏族人一般无二带有高原特色的红晕让人意识到这对夫妻在这里绝非一年半载了。

原来，丈夫 Klaas Steendam 和妻子 Pia Steendam 来自荷兰，早在 1998 年就来到青海，在这里待了 20 多年了，两个儿子也是从小在青海长大的。他们一家甚至能称得上是地道的青海人了。而说起这家店，就不得不说起这对荷兰夫妇在中国的创业故事。

和很多向往中国生活、探索中国奥秘的年轻外国人不同，Klaas 夫妇在 20 世纪 90 年代末来到中国的原因很简单，也很朴素——帮助世界上需要帮助的人。青海省属于中国的欠发达地区，在 20 多年前很少有外国人选择长期待在青海。那时，远在荷兰的 Klaas 还很年轻，正在学习做生意和市场营销。Klaas 家中都是做生意的，所以希望他将来能够接管家族企业。但是，年轻的 Klaas 看到父亲十分忙碌，把所有的时间、精力都用到挣钱上，他并不想要这样的生活。在认识妻子Pia后，Klaas了解到社会发展研究专业毕业的Pia想要走出荷兰，去帮助世界其他地方需要帮助的人。这时，Klaas认为自己可以和Pia一起，利用自己的商业技能去帮助别人。于是，他们来到了青海。

说起在中国青海创业的故事，Pia说最初根本没想到要去做这件事，而是一件小小的事情改变了他们在中国的工作。1998年初到青海时，夫妻俩学习汉语的同时做过不同的创业尝试。突然有一天，一位藏族大学生来到了他们的家中。原来这个学生从别处听说有外国人要做帮助当地人的事之后，想请他们去自己家乡的村子看一看。Klaas夫妇就和同伴一起从西宁坐大巴车去那个大学生的村庄。20多年前的青海，很多偏远的山村缺少抵达村子的公共汽车。Klaas夫妇和同伴们坐了十个小时的大巴后，

还要坐拖拉机到山谷的深处，路途十分遥远、艰辛。到了村庄后，Klaas 夫妇通过走访、调查，发现那个村子不仅偏远而且十分贫穷，没有基础设施，例如学校、道路。当地只盛产羊毛和牦牛毛。这两样东西因为直接卖给中间商，并不赚钱。“不过，他们用羊毛织的物品具有强烈的藏族风格，非常吸引人。”Pia 提到当时的一个感受，说：“在交流中我们发现他们很擅长编织，也很会挑选羊毛。”于是 Klaas 夫妇决定帮助这个村子里的村民做羊毛或牦牛毛编织的手工艺品。

他们最开始只打算负责技术方面的培训，让村民们自己销售产品。但经过一段时间后，Klaas 夫妇发现在技术方面其实只需

要引导他们规范化，藏民们本身的创意和技艺都很不错，反而是产品的销售是一个大问题。村子里的藏民们大部分一生都没有进过城，更不知道怎么把自己的东西卖出去。如果要帮助他们，就必须帮忙解决销售的问题。于是，Klaas夫妇把工作的重点转到了寻找销售渠道和消费群体的方向上。为此，他们成立了现在这家藏族手工艺编织品公司。也就是从这个村子开始，Klaas夫妇开始了创业之路，之后又延伸到其他村庄。目前，Klaas夫妇的公司已经和四个当地村庄形成稳定的合作关系，也帮助这些村庄的人们增加了收入。

在创业过程中，Pia特别强调了公司鼓励藏族的女性参与到挑选羊毛、编织产品的过程中。因为在藏族文化中，通常是男人缝纫和做衣服。让藏族的女性参与到这个工作中，不仅可以有更多参与生产的人，更重要的是，Pia认为经济欠发达地区女性获得经济收入是非常重要的。事实证明，他们做了一个明智的决定。最初他们销售这些女村民做的产品时，以为很多顾客买这些产品是为了支持女性脱贫。但很快他们发现，女村民们做的产品设计本身就非常吸引人。客人们既想支持、帮助这些村民，又被这些美丽的手工艺品吸引。其实，在中国广袤的土地上，也有很多类似的带有公益性质的企业在支持着欠发达地区女性的成长。这些企业的发展不仅仅是因为消费者愿意支持这些女性，还因为这些女性设计、生产的产品确实打动了消费者。

最开始的时候，只有一些来西宁旅游的外国游客购买他们的产品。后来，Klaas夫妇和村民们合作的产品类别越来越多，兼具美观和实用，吸引了越来越多的中国游客进店购买。现在，Klaas夫妇店里最大的消费群体就是来自中国北京、上海等城市的大批量的游客。当然，最让他们感到自豪的是当地藏族人也会购买他们的产品。Pia展示了一款斜着背的，长长的、桶状的包包，上面是蓝色传统藏族风格的编织花纹。这是他们店里最热销的一款产品，不仅外国和中国游客喜欢，就连许多西宁本地人也很喜欢。而这款产品恰恰是长期和Klaas夫妇合作的一

位牧民设计的。只要给予这些村民们展示的机会，他们会让大家看到他们的创意和手工是如此的出色。

尽管初来青海创业的过程并不是那么顺利，生活也非常的艰苦，但Klaas夫妇并没有一丝后悔。回忆起20多年前一家人住在一个小村子中学里的生活时，Klaas至今仍然记得房屋没有卫生间也没有自来水，在冬天的早上如果想要洗脸，他们一家人必须要花很大的工夫把冰融化掉才能烧水洗脸。Klaas说："那时的生活真是艰苦啊。"可是，从全世界海拔最低的荷兰来到世界海拔最高的中国青海，Klaas和Pia在这里寻找到人生的意义，帮助了当地的村民，也成就了自己的事业。在他们看来，这里的生活和之前在荷兰的生活很不一样，但更有意义。在中国创业，既是Klaas夫妇人生的新起点，也是他们实现人生抱负的目标。

Scan for a Video

久久不见久久见

Seeing Old Friends

Seeing Old Friends

Located in Qionghai City in the southernmost province of Hainan in China, the Wanquan Lake is surrounded by green mountains enshrouded in white clouds. Accompanied by a group of young people of different races, a gentle woman takes the ferry across the lake to a village of Miao ethnic group in Huishan Town. She wears a blue blouse and a wide-brimmed hat. Why are these people going to visit this remote village in Hainan? Our story begins with this American woman named Elizabeth.

Sent by the Missouri State University in 2004, Elizabeth worked as an English teacher at North China University of Science and Technology in Tangshan City, Hebei Province. She planned to teach for one year, but during her stay she became captivated by Chinese culture. After she visited Hainan, she did not want to leave, and ended up settling down in China for 15 years.

Elizabeth is embarrassed about the pre-conceived notions she had of China before she came. In fact, she actually thought Chinese men still wore long hair braided in the back. When she got off the plane in Beijing in 2004, however, she was astonished at the modern cosmopolitan city before her eyes. She uses the word "modern" twice in her remarks describing China. Like many foreigners, Elizabeth only knew something about China based on what she'd heard before she came. Only after she'd arrived could she discover its charm.

As they disembark the ferry, Elizabeth and her friends are warmly welcomed by local villagers, who are clapping their hands and shouting, "Here comes our old friend!" in the Hainan dialect. Why is Elizabeth considered an old friend in this remote village? It turns out that when Elizabeth came to Hainan in 2007, she'd decided to stay because she was impressed by the local culture and landscape. Over the years, she has made frequent trips to the village, bringing many foreigners here for visits and offering a lot of help to the local villagers and has become their good friends. Elizabeth is taken to an awning to sit. A Miao elderly person tells her to wear a headdress. Elizabeth doesn't understand the dialect, but can easily know what the elderly person means. She accepts the headdress, and the elderly person puts it on her head and pats her shoulders. The red headdress is embroidered with pretty flowers. Elizabeth is so happy to wear it.

Elizabeth came to visit her old friends and also expose these young people from different countries to the local art — Miao embroidery. The villagers take them to a courtyard in front of a house. The young people sit on small stools, watching local women make the Miao embroidery. The women confidently display their skills and dexterity. This is a harmonious scene of artistic beauty. Elizabeth holds one piece of semi-finished embroidery and talks about it with the group. An elderly woman sees this and shows them a piece of finished Miao embroidery, explaining that it is a decoration for a sleeve. Elizabeth cannot help saying, "This is a high-level skill. From the way it [the stitch] exchanges, you can tell it's Miao." It features symmetrical patterns embroidered with colorful thread. Miao embroidery is well-known throughout China and epitomizes the history of the development of the Miao ethnic group. Elizabeth's understanding of Miao history and culture explains why she so admires Miao embroidery.

True friendship is formed through mutual admiration and respect. This is what Elizabeth has realized through her

interactions with the villagers over the years. She stresses that "there is no need for us to change their lifestyle because they lack nothing and live a happy life." This shows Elizabeth's gentle, equal and respectful attitude towards making friends. It is because of this attitude that she adapts to the village culture and life. She regards the villagers as family and friends. She has also organized medical teams to visit the village and provide medical services, such as physical exams for the elderly. She does not consider herself as their benefactor, but simply as the friend who does what she can. During this trip, Elizabeth meets with an elderly woman over 90 years old. Seeing Elizabeth, the elderly woman begins to stroke her hair and touch her head as if she were her own child. Then she pulls Elizabeth close to her, and nestles her head against Elizabeth's shoulder. Elizabeth does the same. The elderly woman suffers from dementia, so she forgets many people and things, but she still remembers her foreign girl. This shows that equality and sincerity win love and friendship.

Elizabeth does more than just communicate with these villagers, and she also helps spread their culture beyond Hainan. She knows the Hainan local culture, including many local legends and stories. For example, she likes "The Little Dragon Daughter" and "The Story about the Child Called Ao". She has also studied the ancient pottery salvaged from the sea near Hainan. She says that the ancient pottery salvaged here proves that the South China Sea belongs to Hainan and China for thousands of years. While saying this, Elizabeth begins singing a Hainan folk song called "Long Time No See, Long Time See", "Although

we haven't seen each other for a long time, my heart is still open to you ...." The song ends, but tones linger in the air. Elizabeth is moved and says, "The song basically tells that I love you and respect you, and your culture is wonderful." She tells us that her Hainan friends gave her the most beautiful compliment she had ever received in her life. They told me, "Elizabeth, we think maybe in a previous life, you lived in Hainan and were a native Hainanese. In this life, you've come home." After saying these words, Elizabeth dabs her tearful eyes with her silk scarf, and she is shy, but happy.

Elizabeth once thought that Chinese men still wore long plaits. Now she is very familiar with Chinese culture and has such close friends that she considers them as her family. Her story shows that sincerity and kindness will win us friends and love no matter where we are.

久久不见久久见

这里白云低垂到似乎靠在了青山之上，这里青山相拥围成了一片清澈碧绿的万泉湖水，这里“欸乃”一声木桨荡开碧波，这里是中国最南端的省份——海南省的琼海市万泉湖。一位和蔼可亲的外国女士穿着青天蓝的防晒衣，戴着宽檐帽，在一群肤色不同的年轻人的簇拥下乘船穿过万泉湖——他们将要去往会山镇的一个苗族村落。他们是去参观旅游吗？他们为何会来到中国海南这个遥远的少数民族村落呢？这一切都要从来自美国的伊丽莎白说起。

伊丽莎白在2004年的时候受美国密苏里州立大学的派遣，来到中国河北理工大学担任英语外教。她原本只打算在中国待一年，但很快她就被中国文化吸引，到了海南后她就彻底挪不动脚步了。于是，她在中国待了15年。说起她到中国之前，伊丽莎白有些不好意思地回忆："15年前首次在北京下飞机，我以为中国男士的头发都很长，梳成一条辫子挂在身后。但到北京后我完全震惊了。2004年的北京已经是一个完完全全的现代……现代大都市了。"她连用了两个"现代"来表达当时自己对中国面貌的震惊。其实，和很多外国朋友一样，伊丽莎白来中国前对中国的认识仅限于听说，只有当她走近后才意识到这个国度是多么的迷人。

伊丽莎白和年轻的朋友们一下船就受到当地村民的热情欢迎。他们拍着手，用海南话高呼"老朋友"。这是怎么回事呢？偏僻的苗族村落的村民们怎么和伊丽莎白成为老朋友了呢？原来，2007年时伊丽莎白来到海南就被当地的文化和美景所震惊，留了下来。在这期间，她和苗族村落的村民们往来

频繁，带领许多渴望了解中国的外国朋友前来参观交流，她也关怀、帮助当地村民，和村民们结下了深厚的友谊。进村之后，伊丽莎白在当地的老朋友们赶紧拉她到凉棚里坐下，一个苗族老人用苗话说着“戴上这个头巾”，捧着苗绣的传统头巾要为伊丽莎白戴上。虽然伊丽莎白并不太懂苗话，但多年的交往让她马上明白老人的意思，惊喜地双手接过头巾。热情的老人毫不客气地直接给伊丽莎白戴上，并拍拍她的肩膀。这是一块很漂亮的红色苗族头巾，上面用传统的苗绣技艺绣着小花。伊丽莎白激动到举起微握的双手，像个小孩子一样。

这一次重返村子，伊丽莎白不仅是来看望自己的老朋友，还带了一群来自五湖四海的年轻人来欣赏美丽的苗族艺术——苗绣。村民们知晓伊丽莎白的来意后，带着她一起坐到屋前的院子里，现场做起了苗绣。就在简陋的院坝里，展示苗绣技艺的女性们自信、坦然，充满笑容，欣赏苗绣的外国年轻人们自然地坐在低矮的小板凳上，专注地看着她们，这是多么和谐而充满艺术美的一幕。为了让年轻人们真正感受到苗绣的美，伊丽莎白拿起一块半成品向年轻人们讲解，而旁边的老人家看见后，开心地将自己做好的一块绣品搭在伊丽莎白的手臂上，示意这块绣品应该是衣袖的装饰。伊丽莎白不禁感叹："这是一门高超的技艺。从这些交织的针法中一眼就能看出是苗族的作品。"是呀，苗绣是中国重要的绣法之一，强调五色彩线绣成对称的几何图案，并且藏着苗族发展的历史。伊丽莎白对苗绣的欣赏和尊重正是看到、懂得了这个民族的历史文化。

真正的友谊是欣赏，是尊重，也是平等相待，这是伊丽莎白这15年在中国和村民们往来获得的体会。当她谈到自己的这些中国朋友时，她强调："他们什么都不缺，他们过得很开心。我们不需要去改变他们。”这就是伊丽莎白平和、平等、尊重的交友态度。也正是她的这个态度，让她这个外国人融入了村落的文化和人情。她像对待自己的亲人朋友一样，关注到村民们也许需要更贴心的医疗护理，于是她在带着年轻人们来这里欣赏艺术品的同时，也会组织医疗队为苗寨送医送药，帮老人家们检查身体。但她从不以施恩者自居，而是觉得自己只是做了一个朋友该做的事情。这一次，在她要离开村子和大家告别前，她来到一位 90 岁高龄的老奶奶家。老奶奶一看见她就像看见自己的孩子一样，用手捋了捋伊丽莎白的头发，摸摸她的头，然后把她拉到自己面前，把自己的头靠在伊丽莎白的肩上。伊丽莎白也开开

心心地靠上去。这位老奶奶患了健忘症，忘了许多人和事，但仍然记得多年来一直来看她的外国囡囡。只有真诚和平等的心互相贴近，才能够让爱和友谊永存。

伊丽莎白在海南的生活和工作除了与当地村民们交流，还学习和宣传当地文化。她接触了许多海南当地的文化，也熟悉海南的传说和故事。例如，伊丽莎白很喜欢海南岛传说中小龙女和孩子鳌的故事。她还对一些海南打捞的古代瓷器有一定研究。伊丽莎白认为，“这些瓷器足以证明南海属于海南，属于中国，自古以来就是如此。”说着，伊丽莎白用海南话唱起了歌曲《久久不见久久见》。“虽然我们很久没见面了，但我的心一直为你敞开……”一曲终了，余音绕梁。特别容易感动的伊丽莎白深情地说：“我喜欢你，我珍重你，这样的文化实在太棒了。我的海南朋友曾对我说，那是我此生听过的最感动的话语——‘伊丽莎白，也许上辈子你生活在海南，是土生土长的海南人。这辈子，你回家了’。”说完，伊丽莎白用丝巾挡住自己充盈了泪光的眼睛，带着点娇羞快乐的样子。

曾经的伊丽莎白以为中国男人还留着长辫子，而现在的伊丽莎白已经对中国的文化典故非常熟悉，并在这里结交到她足以称之为家人的朋友。伊丽莎白用行动告诉我们，只要怀着一颗真诚友善的心，就可以在一个陌生的国度成为受欢迎的人。

Scan for a Video

一封寄往马里的家书

A Letter to Mali

A Letter to Mali

It is winter in Beijing. The leaves are long gone. Bicycles are lined up neatly on both sides of the road as cars speed by. A tall figure in blue walks steadily to the university building despite the cold wind. He enters a classroom, takes off his coat, and sits down quietly. He takes out a pen and some paper from his bag. He looks healthy, but his eyes betray homesickness. His name is Moise, and he is from Mali.

One year ago, Moise came to study in Beijing. Like any overseas student away from home, he encountered many difficulties adapting to life in a foreign country. His integration was particularly hard, however, as we can see from the letter he sent to his parents back in Africa.

Like most overseas students, his letter begins by saying that all is well. "Dear Mom and Dad, it has been a year since I left home. I miss you and everyone else in the family. Please don't worry about me. I have gradually adapted to university life in China." However, he cannot

help revealing his worries in his letter. He goes on to say that Beijing is much different from what he is used to thinking about, and so large that it is hard to live. When walking down the street, he watches the crowds coming and going, and feels that people are indifferent to one another. In his hometown, people often greet one another as they meet. But in Beijing, people go by too quickly, never stopping to greet one another. The maze-like subway system is also confusing to him. Consequently, he does not dare to go out alone. Moise suffers a bit more than others because he is shy and introverted, and reluctant to greet others in this strange city, let alone ask for help.

However, Moise mentions one thing that makes him feel warm in the cold winter, which would become his first step in beginning to open up to others. Since he comes from a warm part of Africa, he feels extremely cold in Beijing. When he saw the pond beside the school library frozen for the first time, he stood there for a long time, touching the icy surface with his feet when no one watched. He repeatedly describes the frozen pond to his parents in the letter, and how it made him think of the story of Jesus walking on the water in the Gospel of Mark in the Bible. It made him think that people also had the ability to do miracles just like Jesus. Unfortunately, however, the cold wind and air caused Moise to catch a cold. He tried to tough it out at first, but his runny nose and fever forced him to the school clinic. It was there that a student named Yang helped him get his prescription. Suddenly, Moise felt that he was cared for. He writes about this moving help in his letter, telling his parents that a student named Yang helped him, and Yang was a Chinese surname, and how grateful and lucky he was in meeting Yang.

After receiving his help, Moise got to know Yang. This growing friendship helped Moise dismantle his social barriers, urging him to venture out more, and explore the university and Beijing. He began greeting those he knew with a smile like other overseas students. When he said hello, he found that they would also smile and greet him just like people in his hometown. His favorite place to go was the football stadium. Back home, he always enjoyed playing football and running together and cooperating with his teammates. But during his first several months in Beijing, he would only watch, still feeling shy and afraid that other students wouldn't want to play with him. But now he was feeling differently, and this became apparent when one day a football flew towards him from the field. His desire to play football, dormant for so long, was immediately re-ignited. He skillfully kicked the ball back into the field and got a big round of applause from the other players. As he was about to leave, two players ran up to him and invited him to play. From that point on, he has become a frequent player seen on the field. When speaking about this, he smiles. He tells his parents in his letter, "I really enjoy playing with them."

Over time, Moise began to open his mind to new experiences, such as meeting with Yang and some football players to drink milk tea. Drinking milk tea was something new to him as he had never tried it before, and he was a bit worried that it might taste strange. However, curiosity got the better of him. From the first moment he drank it, he knew that he loved it. This led to a continuation of trying more new things, like learning how to shop online, which he did with the help of a classmate. "The delivery is so fast," he thought when he received the delivery message to pick up his package. He went to the delivery area and observed other students get their packages. Though the delivery staff tried to help him, he couldn't understand, so they both had to use gestures to communicate. But this didn't bother him, and in fact he smiles when he talks about it. He understood that there were many people just like him who are learning new things. After receiving his first package, he was very proud. When he writes about this in his letter, he can't help asking his parents, "Shouldn't I be proud of this?"

Over the past year, Moise has gradually realized that even though they don't share the same religion, Chinese people are ready to help others despite cultural or language differences. Their characteristics of kindness and friendliness are just like those found in other countries, including his homeland. He has slowly been writing his own story of studying in China, and through his experiences he continues to acquire a better understanding of China. More than this, however, is how he is acquiring a better understanding of himself. This he also tells his parents in his letter.

一封寄往马里的家书

北京的寒冬，已经冷到街上没有一片树叶了。光秃秃的街道两边整整齐齐地排列着自行车，马路上的汽车飞驰而过。一个高大的蓝色身影出现在这条道路上，顶着寒风往教学楼走去。他找到一个教室，脱下外套，安安静静地坐下来，从包里掏出了纸和笔。他黝黑的皮肤看起来健康自然，可漂亮的双眼皮下却流露着思念的目光。他就是来自马里的Moise。

Moise一年前以留学生的身份来到中国北京留学。和很多来中国留学或者从中国去国外留学的学生一样，Moise面临着如何融

入这个陌生的国度的问题。但比起别的留学生或者别的在中国的外国人，他的融入格外艰难。也许，我们能从他给远在非洲的父母写的信中了解原因。

和所有的留学生一样，Moise在信的开头都是报平安——“亲爱的爸爸妈妈，我离家已经一年了，我一直挂念你们还有其他家人。请不要为我担心，我已经逐渐适应了这里的大学生活”。但实际上，他在信中也忍不住流露一些惶恐。对于Moise来说，北京真的太大了，是一个全然不同的地方。走在大街上的时候，Moise看着来来往往、川流不息的人群，觉得他们似乎彼此漠不关心。可是，Moise想到在自己的家乡，大家都熟悉彼此，会互相问候。而北京的人们步履匆匆，看上去从不愿意停下来和人打招呼。对于Moise来说，北京的地铁系统简直就是迷宫，常常让他分不清方向。这让Moise直到现在都不敢独自出门。当然，Moise如此煎熬还在于他是一个十分内向、害羞的男孩。他很难、甚至不敢在这个陌生的城市主动和别人打招呼，寻求帮助。

但是，Moise在信中笔锋一转，提到了一件让他在北京的冬天感受到温暖、尝试着迈出交流第一步的事情。北京的冬天对于来自温暖非洲的Moise来说实在是太冷了。第一次看到图书馆旁边的池塘结冰冻住的时候，Moise在旁边站了半天，趁着别人没注意的时候偷偷用脚去碰了碰。他在写给父母的家书中反复描写结冰的池塘，甚至联想到马可福音中描写的耶稣光着脚在水面上行走的神迹。在Moise看来，在这种厚厚的冰层上，人们甚至可以做和耶稣同样的神迹之事。不幸的是，北京户外的寒风太大、气温太低，Moise感冒了。原本他想忍一忍，可鼻涕和头痛让他不得不鼓足勇气走进校医院。正是在校医院里，东张西望的Moise得到了一位姓杨的男同学的帮助，开到了感冒药。这时，Moise意识到自己并不是不被人关注，也不是没有人关心的。Moise将这激动人心的援助写进了信里，告诉爸爸妈妈“杨是中国的一个姓”，尽力表达自己遇到杨同学的感激和幸运。

从认识杨同学、得到杨同学的帮助开始，Moise尝试着放下隔膜去感受学校和北京这座城市，尝试着去理解而不是逃避。他开始像别的留学生那样，遇到认识的同学会主动微笑打招呼。当他打招呼的时候，他发现同学们也会冲他微笑，就像他在家乡时一样。Moise最喜欢逛的地方还是足球场。他在家乡的时候就喜欢踢足球，喜欢和同伴们一起合作、奔跑的感觉。但来了中国几个月，他的进步还仅限于远远驻足观看。他还是那么害羞，担心踢足球的同学们不会接纳他这个陌生人。可是有一次，当他驻足的时候，场上的足球正好飞到他的面前。那一刻，蛰伏许久的热情被突如其来的这颗球点燃，他的冲动超越了他的羞怯和犹豫。Moise用娴熟的一脚将足球踢回了场上，赢得了踢球的同学们的喝彩。当Moise正准备离开时，两个男同学跑过来，用英文热切地邀请Moise一起去踢球。从此以后，Moise和这群同学一样成为了足球场上的常客。当提到这件事时，Moise笑起来，他给父母写道："我真的很享受与他们的比赛。"

在中国，在北京，Moise慢慢地打开了心扉。在和球队的朋友们、杨同学熟悉后，Moise会和他们一起去喝奶茶。对他来说，第一次喝奶茶真是新奇又担心。在家乡，他没有喝过这种饮料，担心味道会很奇怪，但与此同时，他的内心又十分雀跃。在奶茶小哥递上奶茶时，他迫不及待地和同学们一起插上吸管大大地喝了一口，第一口就让Moise爱上了这种奶和茶混搭的饮料。他开始和中国学生一起去尝试一些对他来说非常特别的事物。Moise写到在中国尝试新事物时，又向父母提到自己已经学会网购了。第一次在朋友帮助下下单网购后，没多久Moise就收到了取包裹的信息。对他来说，包裹来得真快啊！Moise决定自己一个人去快递点取包裹。他到了快递点后，习惯性地先观察别的同学取包裹的程序。旁边的快递点的工作人员看到后，非常友善地用中文教他，可Moise的中文表达也不够地道，两人就手舞足蹈了一番。但那一刻，Moise笑得很开心。因为他知道，自己在学习新东西的时候不是一个人。取到第一个快递后，Moise在内心给自己点了一个赞。甚至在给父母写信说到这件事情的时候，性格羞涩的Moise竟然忍不住写了一句："我值得骄傲吗？"

Moise在中国生活的这一年使他渐渐认识到，中国和自己的家乡很不一样，中国的大部分人甚至和他信仰的宗教不一样，但是当自己需要帮助时，这些人就会伸出援助之手。他们的友善、亲切和热情和世界上其他国家、和Moise的祖国马里是一样的。Moise在一点一滴的中国留学生活中书写着自己的故事，去经历、认识对自己来说还是颇为陌生的中国。但他坚信，自己在这里可以迈出第一步，可以获得成长。他也是这样在信中告诉他的父母的。

Scan for a Video

乘着“一带一路”的东风到中国

Coming to China Thanks to the Belt and Road Initiative

Coming to China Thanks to the Belt and Road Initiative

During the winter in Beijing, most vegetable shops stack their Chinese cabbages on the outermost edges of their stalls so that customers can select several at once. One day, a foreign young man with deep-set eyes who was wearing a brown leather jacket walked into a shop and patted a Chinese cabbage. The female shopkeeper was worried how she could help him, assuming that he could not speak Chinese. Unexpectedly, he raised the cabbage and asked loudly in Chinese, "How much is this cabbage? Do you have any tomatoes?" The shopkeeper smiled and came over to greet him. The young man talked with her fluently in Chinese and then bought a cabbage and some tomatoes and eggplants. The young man is Jaml Afzal from Pakistan.

Jaml is 25 years old, and he is an overseas student at the Communication University of China. He came to China to study Chinese. His hometown is Chitta Batta in northern Pakistan. China

and Pakistan have maintained good diplomatic relations. It is not so surprising to see Pakistani students speak fluent Chinese in Beijing. But Jaml thinks that his experience of coming to China to study Chinese is very unique.

“I am a mama's boy,” he says, meaning that he is very dependent on and easily swayed by his mother and obeys her word. Why does he use such a Chinese phrase to describe himself? It is used to express that he is quite attached to his family and rather unwilling to leave. Before he came to study in China, Jaml was reluctant to part with his mother, and even said that he would not study abroad without her permission. However, though his mother told him not to study abroad, Jaml still came to China, knowing that it was a precious opportunity. His family also understands what a precious opportunity it is. During phone calls home, his father always asks if he is taking his study seriously.

When he first came to China, Jaml felt that he'd made a mistake. He missed his family greatly and did not enjoy studying Chinese. In the beginning, he only knew the Chinese for "hello" and "uncle", and could not understand the teacher in class. He found Chinese pronunciation very difficult to learn, such as being able to distinguish between the similar-sounding Chinese words for *xifu* "daughter-in-law" and *xifu* "costume". But every time he felt discouraged, his family would encourage him by saying, "You must study Chinese conscientiously because it is a very important language and you need this language later in Pakistan as well." Jaml says that his family has been very supportive and encouraging. Now he can speak Chinese fluently.

His family's eagerness for Jaml to learn Chinese well is due in large part to China's implementation of the Belt and Road Initiative which was proposed by Chinese President Xi Jinping in 2013. By borrowing the historical symbol of the ancient Chinese Silk Road, the Initiative calls for China and countries along the ancient trade route to cooperate together to create a community of shared interests, of a shared future, and of shared responsibility featuring political mutual trust, economic integration, and cultural inclusiveness. Jaml's hometown is Chitta Batta in northern Pakistan, and it is an important construction site for the China-Pakistan Trade Corridor as planned in the Belt and Road Initiative. China and Pakistan have already completed the "1+4" cooperation layout which concentrates on Gwadar Port, energy, transportation infrastructure, and industrial parks. This layout will affect three billion people and help promote the economic development of many regions along the Belt and Road. There are more than 30 construction projects in the China-Pakistan Economic Corridor which will create countless new jobs. Jaml says that the number of jobs has increased in his hometown and everyone has a new source of income. Before he came to China, the construction of the

China-Pakistan Economic Corridor enabled him to see many Chinese people. He saw Chinese workers devoted to their jobs, working in 24-hour shifts and enduring hardships. “We were moved by the hard-working spirit of these Chinese workers,” Jaml says. He often thinks of this hard-working spirit while studying Chinese. He says it is because of the Belt and Road Initiative that he came to China, and that his family urged him to study Chinese well so that he could return home to help build his hometown to create more opportunities. It is easy to understand that even though his family was so reluctant to part with Jaml, they still sent him to China to study Chinese.

Studying in China helps Jaml and many foreigners acquire a new understanding of China. While in Pakistan, he was impressed by the hard-working spirit of Chinese workers, and after living in China he saw that Chinese people can endure hardships, are hard-working, are good at planning their study and work, and make good use of their spare time. Jaml also began to think of how he could seek personal development and be more actively involved in the Belt and Road Initiative. In 2019, he seized the opportunity to participate in the Belt and Road Documentary Forum held in Beijing. He was eager to learn

more about the Belt and Road Initiative and how it was viewed by Chinese people and foreigners. He found many outstanding foreign participants at the forum who wanted to be involved in the Belt and Road Initiative in China and had their own unique views about it. He also found many other young people just like him who are eager to learn more about it and participate in its construction. He says he wants to be a part of the exciting wave of the times, along with all these other outstanding people. "The Belt and Road Documentary Forum showcases China's diplomatic event at home," says Jaml. It enabled more people to see China's vision of peaceful development and shared prosperity. More and more young people have been becoming attracted to China and want to come to study and conduct exchanges. At the forum, in fluent Chinese Jaml asked for a drink and talked with another young participant.

It is thanks to the Belt and Road Initiative that Jaml has come to China to study Chinese, and it may be because of the Belt and Road Initiative that he will be able to return to Pakistan to contribute to the future economic development of his home country.

乘着“一带一路”的东风到中国

北京的蔬菜店在冬天的时候大多会把白菜摆在摊位的最外沿，方便居民们一口气捡上好几个装袋。一个穿着棕色皮衣短外套、眉目深邃的外国小伙子走进蔬菜店，拍了拍最外沿的白菜。卖菜的阿姨犯愁了，咋办，这小伙子看起来不是很会中文的样子。没想到这个小伙子举起白菜，大声地用中文问：“白菜怎么卖？有西红柿吗？”阿姨一下笑了，赶紧上前招呼。小伙子用中文流利地和阿姨对话，不一会儿就买上了白菜、西红柿和茄子。这个用中文熟练买菜的小伙子是来自巴基斯坦的Jaml Afzal。

Jaml今年25岁，是中国传媒大学的一名留学生，来中国学习汉语。他的家乡在巴基斯坦北部的Chitta Batta。中国和巴基斯坦的外交关系一直保持得比较好，在北京看到中文说得流利的巴基斯坦留学生也就不那么令人惊讶了。但在Jaml看来，自己来中国学习汉语的经历是非常独特的。

“我是一个妈宝男。”Jaml这样评价自己。在中文的语境里，“妈宝男”意味着男孩十分依赖自己的母亲，没有主见，事事都听母亲的。为什么Jaml要用这样一个中文词来形容自己呢？原来，他是想表达自己非常依恋家人，不愿意离开家庭。当初来中国留学前，Jaml舍不得妈妈，就对妈妈说，

如果你不让我走我就不走。结果妈妈干脆地说，那不要走好了。最后，Jaml仍然是带着对父母的满腔依恋来到中国学习汉语的。他知道，这个机会很珍贵。家里人也知道这个珍贵的机会来之不易，所以即使很思念，爸爸每次通电话的时候都会再问一句："你在认真学汉语吗？"

刚到中国的时候，Jaml怀着对家人的思念和对汉语学习的抗拒，觉得自己来到中国就是一个错误。他只会"你好"和"叔叔"两个词。老师在课堂上的教学让他如坠云里雾里。中文的发音学起来太困难，"媳妇"和"戏服"竟然是两个完全不同的词。可每次觉得特别艰难的时候，家里人都会在电话里安慰他，再加上一句"你必须认真学，因为汉语很重要，你今后在巴基斯坦也能用到，所以你必须好好学"。在Jaml看来，是家里人一直在后面支持、鼓励、推动着自己学汉语，所以现在他才能流利地用汉语和中国人对话。

Jaml一家人都这样迫切地让他学好汉语，很大一部分原因是中国实施的"一带一

路”倡议。“一带一路”是中国习近平主席在2013年提出的，借用中国古代丝绸之路的历史符号，和沿线国家平等合作，打造政治互信、经济融合、文化包容的利益共同体、命运共同体和责任共同体。Jaml的家乡Chitta Batta在巴基斯坦北部，也是“一带一路”中巴贸易走廊的重要建设地。目前，中国和巴基斯坦以中巴经济走廊为核心，已经完成了瓜达尔港、能源、交通基础设施、产业园区为重点的“1+4”合作布局。这个布局和规划覆盖了30亿人口，惠及了沿线很多地区的经济发展，仅在中巴经济走廊的建设内容就超过了30项，创造了无数新的就业岗位。而对于Jaml来说，最直观的感受就是家乡经济就业的岗位增多了，大家有了新的收入来源。同时，中巴经济走廊的建设让他在来中国之前就看到过很多中国人。这些中国工人非常专注于自己的工作，24小时轮班，吃苦耐劳。Jaml说：“我们被中国工人的精神所打动。”说到这里时，Jaml提到自己学习汉语时也是想到了他们的这种精神。Jaml可谓是乘着“一带一路”的东风来到中国的，而家里人督促他学好汉语回去建设家乡也是在“一带一路”的大背景下才有更多发挥的机会。这下我们总算理解了为什么全家人那么舍不得Jaml，却仍然送他来中国学汉语。

Jaml在中国留学期间，他和很多外国人一样，对中国有了新的认识。以前在巴基斯坦的时候，他被中国工人艰苦奋斗的精神所打动。来了中国后，他发现中国人不仅吃苦耐劳、认真工作，他们常常对自己的学业、工作是有规划的，能够很好地利用自己空闲的时间。Jaml在一些中国朋友的影响下，开始在学校学习汉语之外思考如何借助“一带一路”来实现个人的发展。于是，他抓住机会参加了2019年在北京举办的“一带一路”纪录片论坛。他渴望通过这些方式去更多地了解“一带一路”，了解中国人、外国人对“一带一路”的认识和评价。在论坛的现场，Jaml发现参会者有许多优秀的外国人，他们愿意在中国做一番事业，也有自己对“一带一路”独特的看法。Jaml还发现，也有很多和自己一样的年轻人来到这里了解、学习“一带一路”的内容，渴望与那些优秀的人一起参与到时代建设的浪潮中。Jaml认为：“对于‘一带一路’纪录片论坛而言，它是中国主场外交的表现。”这种主场外交让更多的人看到了中国和平发展、

共同繁荣的建设理念，也吸引了更多的年轻人来到更加自信的中国进行学习和交流。Jaml在会场上用流利的汉语向服务员要了一杯牛奶，然后和旁边另一个参会的年轻人用汉语彼此愉快地交流起来。

正是“一带一路”让Jaml带着憧憬和全家人的支持来到中国学习汉语，而Jaml在学汉语的同时也在了解“一带一路”，为将来中巴两国的经济建设积蓄自己的力量。

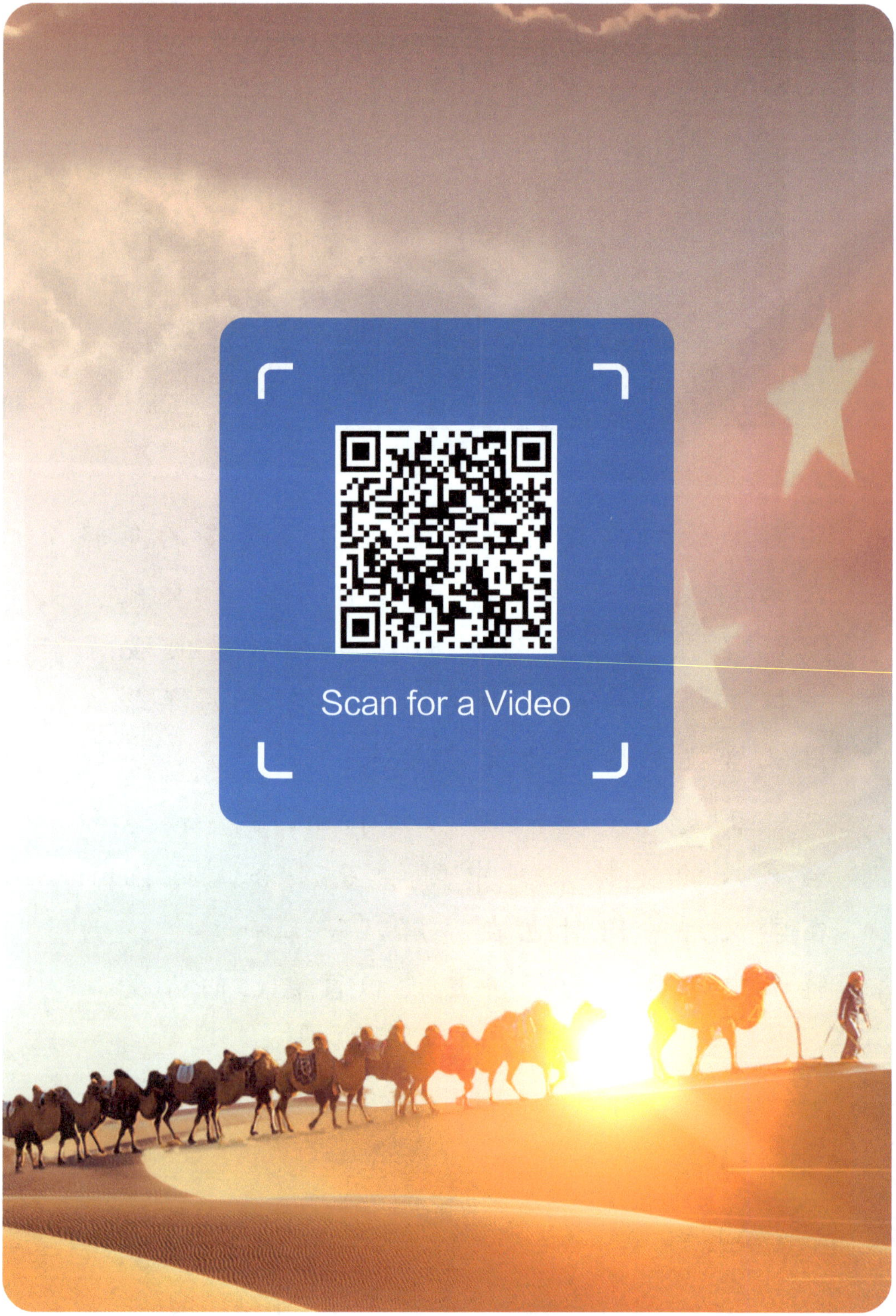
Scan for a Video

在北京重拾旧日时光

Reliving the Old Days in Beijing

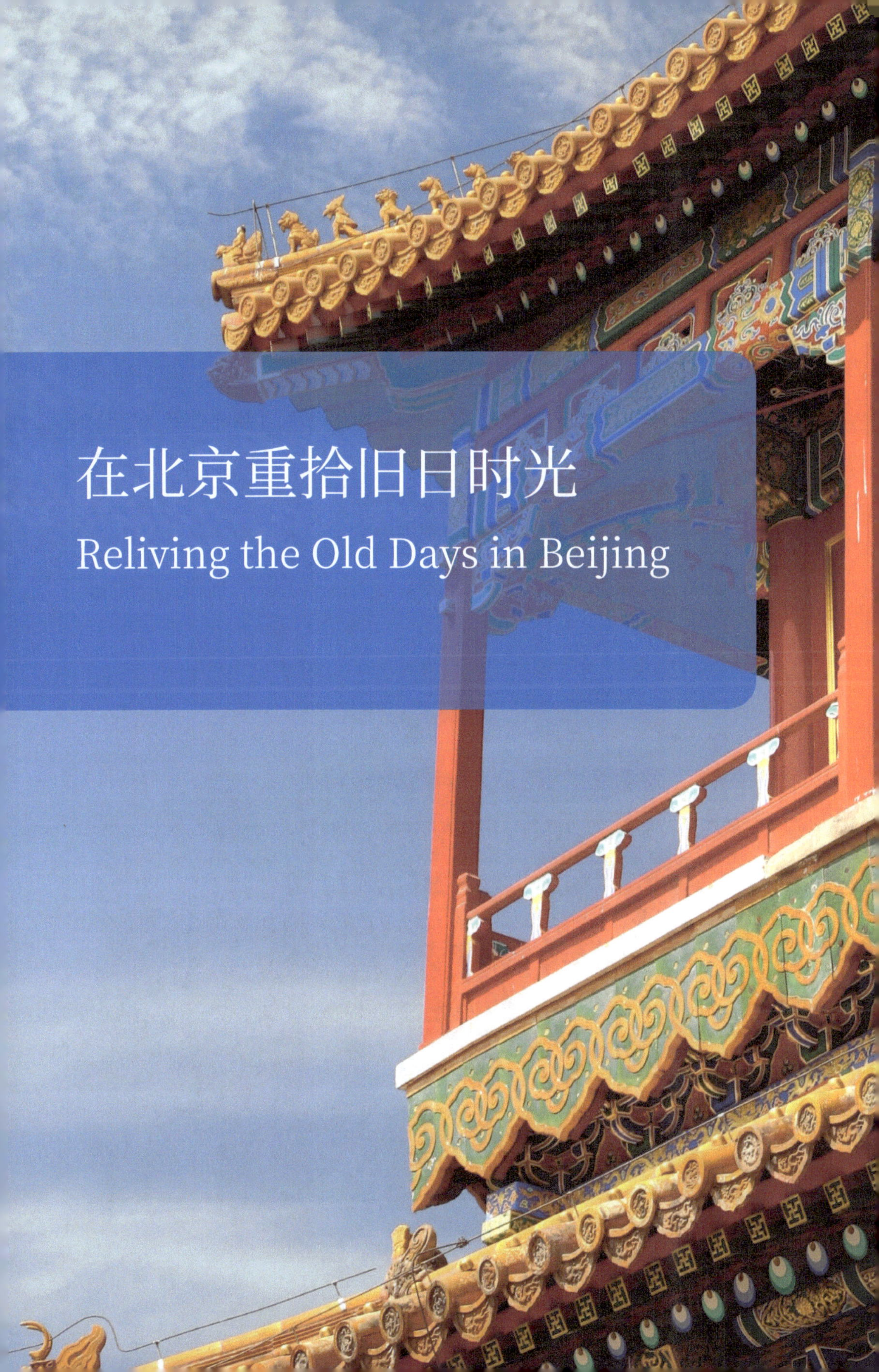

Reliving the Old Days in Beijing

The red walls and black tiles of Yishu 8 on Donghuangchenggen North Street are vibrant under Beijing's blue sky, showing new vitality just like other ancient and modern siheyuans (courtyard houses) in this city. One hundred years ago, it was the site of the Sino-French University, a sister school with the University of Lyon, France. The building has been well-preserved, and it is now a place for art exchanges between China and Europe. It is also the workplace for Capucine, a French architect and artist.

Capucine came to Beijing in 2012 with her husband, also an architect. When I first met Capucine in her studio, she had short hair and was wearing a blue apron, and was moving an old door from one side of the studio to the middle. With her gray-blue eyes, she studied the old

door carefully. Her studio was filled with many different old doors, most of them no longer in their original form, and some with graffiti. This is what Capucine does in Beijing — she collects old doors and creates art from them. To Capucine, old doors are the best way for her to open the door to Chinese culture and talk about Beijing culture.

What Capucine does is reminiscent of what she used to do in Paris. For her, making art out of old doors in Beijing is her own way of reliving the old days, and not just Beijing's past, but also her own past. When she lived in Paris, Capucine also enjoyed reusing old building materials to create art. She says that they give her a lot of inspiration. When she first came to Beijing, she felt curious about everything. But this city, which is both ancient and modern, also made her feel a little strange, and she didn't know what to do. While wandering around Beijing, she saw many new and old buildings harmoniously situated under the same sky, and many old folk doors looked very interesting to her, like recordings of the old days of families in Beijing. It was Beijing itself that inspired her to use these old building materials. In Paris, it was something different. But in Beijing, it was the old doors.

Capucine's studio is filled with them. For her, doors carry the stories of Beijing. They speak to her and give her the idea of "saying" something. Her artistic creations are often based on the style and color of each door and the kind of memories they manifest. Her favorite door is one which is light wood with no paint left, and full of spots and advertisements. These advertisements appear to have been printed with an ink printer, and are clear and square. One reads "professional unclogging and drilling holes," and another reads "seal-engraving, handling certificates and invoices." Capucine likes them very much.

She thinks that this style of graffiti is very Beijing, and shows a piece of the city's history, a piece of its life. In an empty space in the lower left corner of the door, she paints a little girl with downcast eyes. To Capucine, this little girl represents any little girl in Beijing as she walks through the streets and past the houses covered in ads, enjoying her free time after school. Through these artistic creations, Capucine relives her childhood and the old days in Paris. They help her transcend space and time, which makes her happy.

In creating her art, she first measures the door's dimensions and then sketches her idea on some paper. She will not paint directly on the door yet because it is old and worn-out. She will make designs according to the characteristics of the door and the feeling it gives her, and won't begin until she is satisfied with her design. She has black-and-white photos on the table and the wall as sources of inspiration. She buys these photos at flea markets. Many are photos of Chinese people. There are photos of two shy secondary school students wearing scarves and posing side by side, other photos show a family of five in the photography studio, and still others are moments of children laughing. These old black-and-white photos and even their old wooden frames tell stories of Beijing, which gives Capucine a lot of inspiration. A door she recently painted reminds her of an old photo. She quickly finds it. It is a black-and-white photo taken by 19th-century Scottish photographer John Thomson, who came to China and photographed the lives of Chinese people during the Qing Dynasty. It is of a girl in a Qing-Dynasty dress. Capucine shows me the door she designed based on the photo. Inspired by the flowery pattern on a Chinese table cloth, she painted a Chinese woman's scarf on the glass of the door. Beneath the glass is a crimson wood board with a crack in the middle. Here she

created the image of a female head. With this creation, this abandoned old door seems to glow with new vitality. Capucine says that this art is the product of integrating her own French culture she carries with her and her unique encounters with the Chinese culture.

How Capucine finds these old doors is also an interesting story. She would often go to the Sanyanjing Hutong in Beijing, where she'd walk around and find interesting things. When local people asked what she was doing, she would happily respond in fluent Chinese, "I like recycling old doors." Local people would then direct her to houses where they'd changed the doors. Later, she got acquainted with the people on the three-wheeled carts who went around the city gathering things to recycle, and would ask them to help her find old doors. Traveling through the hutongs in Beijing gave Capucine a lot of inspiration. She could see the lifestyle of the local people, and see their faces as she observed their daily lives in the hutongs. After she got acquainted with some women who also enjoyed wandering through the hutongs, Capucine would eat snacks with them and talk. “I like living in Beijing very much,” she says. “People are warm-hearted. When I first came to China, I liked the city very much. China is a country where tradition and modern civilization are intertwined, which gives me inspiration. By creating art from doors, I can tell Europeans how warm Chinese are and talk about my daily life.” These doors in Beijing have given Capucine inspiration to create art, but they've also enabled her to relive her old days. In the studio of Yishu 8, Capucine uses doors to show us a beautiful world, one which was created through the integration of French and Chinese cultures.

在北京重拾旧日时光

北京瓦蓝瓦蓝的天空下，东皇城根北街艺术8的红墙黑瓦显得格外精神，就跟这座城市其他古老又现代的四合院一样焕发着新的生命力。这里原是百年前和法国里昂大学互为姊妹学校的中法大学所在地，历经时光依然保存完好，现在成为中国与欧洲艺术交流之地。来自法国的建筑家、艺术家卡普辛就在这里工作。

2012年，卡普辛随被派到北京工作的建筑师丈夫来到北京。第一次见到卡普辛的时候，她顶着一头男式短发，看起来干净利落。她扎着蓝色的围裙，正把一块老旧的

门板从工作室的一侧搬到正中间。她仔细端详着这块旧门板，灰蓝色的眼珠透着专注和喜爱。她的工作室里摆满了各色各样的旧门板，不少门板已经看不出原来的样子，还有一些门板上的涂鸦充满了儿童的趣味。对！这就是卡普辛在北京的工作——收集旧门板，并在上面创作绘画作品。对卡普辛而言，旧门板是她打开中国文化大门和谈论北京文化的最好方式。

说起收集旧门板进行创作，不得不提起卡普辛曾经在巴黎的工作。对她而言，在北京收集旧门板进行艺术创作是重拾旧日时光，不仅仅是重拾老北京的旧日时光，还是重拾她自己的旧日时光。在巴黎的时候，卡普辛特别喜欢重复利用废旧建筑材料进行艺术创作。这些旧材料给了她很多灵感。初来

北京时，她对北京的一切都感到新鲜又好奇。不过这座古老又现代的城市也让她感

到有些陌生，不知道该在这里做什么。后来，她在北京四处溜达时，看见北京的新旧建筑和谐地处在同一天空下，而很多民间的废旧的门板看起来很有意思，记录着一个北京家庭的旧日时光。正是北京这座城市再次激发了她使用旧材料的想法。这一次，她的注意力被北京的旧门板吸引了。

卡普辛的工作室里堆满了各种样式的旧门板。对卡普辛而言，门板承载着北京故事，它在和她说话，让她产生了一些在门板上面“说”点什么的念头。因此，卡普辛往往是根据每一个门板的样式、色彩及带给她的记忆感觉进行创作。卡普辛最喜欢的门板是一块连漆都没有了只剩下斑点和各种小广告的浅木色门板。这些小广告像是用打印机印上去的一样，清晰、方正，上面多是“专业疏通打孔”“刻章办证发票”等。卡普辛非常喜欢，认为这种涂鸦是非常北京化、非常本土生活化的内容，就像一段生活的纪念品，写满了时间的痕迹。于是，她在门板左下角比较空的地方用墨水创作了一个眉目低垂、正迈着大步走路的小女孩。在卡普辛看来，这个小女孩就是北京街道上任何一个小女孩，她穿过布满各种小广告的街道、人家，自由地享受放学的时光。这个门板和这个小女孩一样，都是自由自在的。而这个门板和创作也再次唤醒了卡普辛自己的童年自由生活。她的童年和巴黎时光隔着空间和时间在北京被重新捡起来，再度给予她欢乐。

卡普辛在旧门板上进行创作的时候会提前用卷尺量好门板的长宽高，然后根据一定的比例画到图纸上。她不会因为门板是破旧的物品就直接随意在上面作画，而是非常慎重。她会根据门板的特征、给她的感觉在脑海里设计，然后落实到图纸上。直到图纸上的设计令她满意了，卡普辛才肯动笔在门板

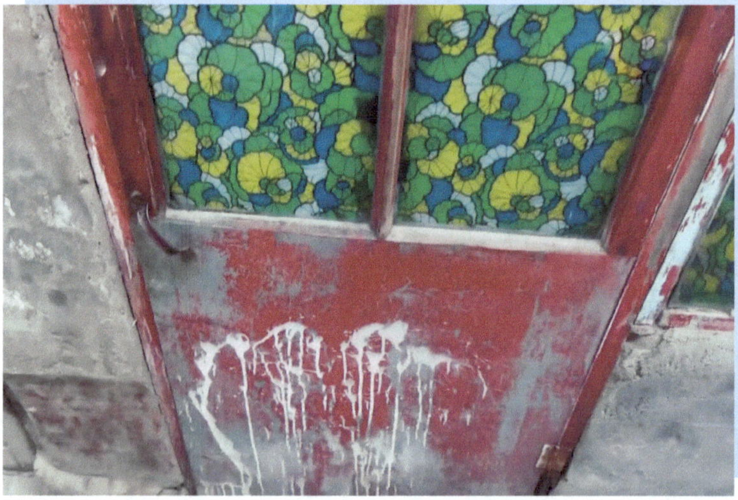

上作画。说到灵感的来源，卡普辛展示了桌上和墙上的黑白照片。这些黑白照片都是卡普辛在旧货市场上买的，上面多是中国人的黑白人像照，有的是两个戴着红领巾的腼腆中学生并肩合影，有的是一家五口专程到照相馆拍照的留念，有的是小朋友在大笑的一瞬间的抓拍……这些黑白旧照片乃至装照片的木框都在讲着北京的故事，给了卡普辛非常多的灵感。卡普辛最近创作的一块门板让她联想到一张旧照片，她很快就找到了，是一张John Thomson拍摄的黑白照片——上面是一个清朝装扮的女孩。John Thomson

是英国较早来中国拍摄黑白照片的摄影师，拍摄了中国清朝时期民间的生活状态。她将中国普通人家常用的餐桌罩的镂空花纹布料设计为女性的头巾，用白色的颜料画在门板的玻璃上。玻璃下方是绛红色的木板，中间已经裂开了一条缝。她在这里设计了一个女性的头像。轮廓出来后，这张被人抛弃的旧门板仿佛焕发了新的生命力。在卡普辛看来，自己带着法国的文化来，遇到中国的文化，彼此融合才成就了这旧门板上的艺术。

说起卡普辛的旧门板艺术创作，就不得不提她去寻找旧门板的故事了。最初，卡普辛常在北京三眼井胡同等地方自己去寻找门板。她会四处逛，顺便发现一些有趣的东西。遇到当地的居民询问她时，她会很开心地用流利的中文表达“我喜欢回收老门”。这时候，一些当地居民就会指点她哪家哪户要换门了。后来，她和一些骑三轮车到处回收东西的人熟悉后，也会请他们帮忙找一些门。在搜集门的过程中，北京的胡同生活也给了卡普辛灵感。她可以在胡同里的日常生活中看到许多生活的颜色、人们的脸和行为。卡普辛在一条胡同里和出门溜达的阿姨们熟悉后，会和阿姨们一起在胡同里吃零食。卡普辛动情地说："我非常喜欢住在北京，人都很好相处。当我第一次来到中国，我就非常喜欢它。它是一个传统和现代文明交织的国家，这些对我来说很有灵感。通过使用门板，我可以告诉欧洲中国多么温暖，也能谈论日常生活。"正是这人间烟火味十足的北京门板，给了卡普辛艺术创作的灵感，也让她重新拾起旧时光里的喜好、记忆。在艺术8的工作室里，卡普辛用门板的创作讲述着法国文化和中国文化融合创造出来的生活的精彩。

Scan for a Video

中国农家乐的三日时光

Three-day "Agri-tainment" in China

Three-day "Agri-tainment" in China

Outside of Beijing in Fangshan District, the first rays of sunlight are shining down on the courtyard of a farmhouse. The door of the courtyard is gently pushed open, and a plainly-dressed farmer comes out with a broom and begins sweeping the fallen leaves on the road blown by the wind during the night. On the other side of the asphalt road, a young figure appears, looking around while walking. His big blue backpack is eye-catching. As he approaches the courtyard, the farmer sees that he is a tall, thin foreign young man. He looks very different from the farmer. A wisp of his short blond hair bounces in front of his forehead like a fashionable young man of the city. His name is Chris, and he is from England.

Unlike many foreigners, Chris has traveled throughout 28 provinces (there are 34 provincial administrative regions) in China and on rivers and mountains all over the country. He has tried many Chinese dishes, and can even distinguish the characteristics of each

of the eight major Chinese cuisines. He especially likes Sichuan cuisine. He also speaks Chinese fluently and can talk easily with Chinese people. This is his first trip to the Chinese countryside, in what he hopes will be the beginning of an idyllic pastoral trip. He, therefore, is looking forward to the three days of "agri-tainment" in this farmhouse.

Nongjiale, or "agri-tainment" in English, means enjoying leisure and entertainment in the countryside, and is a way to enjoy the fun of rural living. Chinese people have appreciated and enjoyed agri-tainment since ancient times. There is a famous ancient poem which asks everyone not to laugh at the muddy, home-brewed wine in the countryside and enjoy the sumptuous dishes served during the harvest season. Chris has traveled through most of China and has acquired a deep understanding of agri-tainment. He is coming here for the pleasure of getting along with the local people and enjoying some rural leisure time.

At the homestay called "Grandma's House", Chris gets acquainted with the housekeepers, three warm-hearted and cheerful middle-aged women. He takes a cue from the local people and calls them "big sisters". Chubby big sister Wei is good at making dumplings, big sister Xu with short hair can make particularly delicious noodles, and big sister Fu with big gold earrings and rings treats Chris to all kinds of delicious food. Their frankness and enthusiasm immediately make Chris feel like he is back home in the English countryside. Big sister Fu develops the closest relationship with him, and when she hears him say that he likes Sichuan cuisine, she doesn't hesitate to offer to introduce him to a Chongqing girl for a blind date, which makes him blush. But he knows that if someone here wants to introduce him to a girl, it means that they can recognize his good character.

On his first day there, Chris learns of the history and is taken by the beauty of this large courtyard. The women tell him that it was built during the Qing Dynasty (1616–1911), and that it has a history of more than a hundred years and represents the traditional residence of rural gentlemen in northern China. The periphery of the courtyard is surrounded by a wall made of irregular stones, with the cracks covered in mud. The stone wall is covered with vines, which looks green and lovely in the summer sunshine. Inside the courtyard there are square houses made of bricks. The doors and windows of the houses are all made of wood, and the window lattices are decorated with traditional Chinese patterns. Chris has seen similar patterns in the Summer Palace and the Forbidden City in Beijing, but the patterns here are simpler and more rustic. To him, such simple and clean houses are charming and warm. The

interior design is modern and minimalist, but also integrates some ancient and modern artwork which gives it a sense of beauty and mystery. Chris feels that it is warm and cozy in this remote part of the Chinese countryside.

On the second day, Chris rises early and goes out to the fields to pick vegetables with the sisters. He comes out to the fields to see that the local people have already begun work, carrying poles with heavy loads. Chinese people are hard-working. Whether in a busy big city or a remote and quiet small village, they all come out early to work. Chris picks red and green peppers from the tops of low pepper seedlings and the long, dangling cowpeas from the tall trellises built with twigs. As the sisters hold picked cucumbers, Chris quickly helps put the cucumbers into the bamboo basket. The vegetables are tender, fresh and natural. After picking vegetables, Chris catches a beetle. Here, pastoral pleasures can be found everywhere. After the hard work, the sisters use the freshly-picked ingredients to make a delicious vegetarian dish: chewy hand-rolled noodles with mouth-watering eggplant gravy. The surface of the fried tofu is golden and crispy, and is plump and juicy on the first bite. The spicy mushrooms are also delicious, and Chris — a big fan of Sichuan cuisine — keeps eating them with his chopsticks. After eating the meal prepared from the food he helped pick, Chris declares, "This journey has refreshed me." Chris sees that China's pastoral countryside is quiet and bountiful. And though it is modern, it is also full of history.

On the third day at Grandma's House, Chris personally prepares a delicious dish from his homeland: English pumpkin soup. In his opinion, there are many English dishes of which Chinese ingredients can be used. Because only the freshest pumpkins make the best flavor, the Chinese countryside pumpkins can be used as they are so fresh. After making the soup, he pours it into hollowed-out small pumpkins, a natural food container. The sisters and some local friends are already sitting at the table quietly waiting as he walks into the dining room, carrying the bowls of pumpkin soup with a happy smile on his face. Besides his pumpkin soup, they also eat some traditional Chinese hand-rolled noodles. The food is very simple and rustic, but it shows deep friendship. While eating the noodles, everyone smiles and talks about how to use chopsticks. This makes Chris once again feel the simplicity and joy of rural life.

Three days in the Chinese farmhouse quickly pass. As Chris says goodbye to everyone, the sisters give Chris some home-grown tomatoes, eggplants, corn, pumpkins and other food. They know that, like them, Chris likes the countryside and the food grown here. "Although we speak different languages and have different cultural backgrounds, we share the same experience with food and the joys and sorrows of life," Chris says. The simplicity, rustic nature and joy of the Chinese pastoral life are the same as those in other countries. People who live in the countryside learn to cherish and enjoy these generous gifts bestowed to them by the land.

中国农家乐的三日时光

当清晨第一缕阳光照下来的时候，中国北京郊区房山的这座农家乐院子一下就敞亮了起来。很快，院子的大门被轻轻推开。穿着朴素的当地人拿着笤帚出来，开始清扫道路上昨夜微风卷下的落叶。在道路的另一头，靠着柏油马路的那边，出现了一个年轻的身影，他一边走一边张望，硕大的蓝色背包十分吸引目光。等他走近这座院子，当地人才发现这是一个高高瘦瘦的外国男孩。他看起来和当地人格外不同，金色的短发在额前留了一绺，有点像城里那些穿着时尚的青年人。他就是来自英国的Chris。

跟许多外国人不一样的是，Chris已经走过了中国的28个省份（中国一共有34个省级行政区），跨越了大江南北很多的江河山川。他品尝过许多中国菜，甚至能够分清楚中国八大菜系中各个菜系的特色，对川菜情有独钟。他的中文也较为流利，能够和中国人流畅地对话。但这是他第一次走进中国的乡村，开启中国乡村田园的旅行。因此，Chris也很期待在这家农家乐将要度过的三天时光。

中文里的“农家乐”是一种在乡村田园中休闲、娱乐的生活方式。这种生活方式是让大家亲近田园，享受农家生活带来的乐趣。中国人自古以来就欣赏、享受农家乐，有一句古诗“莫笑农家腊酒浑，丰年留客足鸡豚”，说的就是请大家不要笑话农村自家酿的酒浑浊，到了丰收的时节待客的菜肴是十分丰盛的。踏遍

大半个中国的Chris是十分理解农家乐的含义的，认为来到这里最大的乐趣就是和当地人相处，在农村的休闲时光中获得快乐。

在北京郊区房山的民宿“姥姥家”，Chris认识的第一批当地人就是民宿的管家们。她们是三位特别热情开朗的阿姨。Chris学着当地人的习惯，称她们为“大姐”。胖胖的魏大姐包得一手好饺子；男式短发的许大姐会做特别好吃的面条；戴着硕大金耳环和金戒指的付大姐的乐趣之一就是请Chris吃各种美味的食物。她们的率直与热情让Chris一下找到了在英国乡下的感觉，像回到家一样。当听到Chris说自己喜欢川菜时，和Chris关系最好的付大姐毫不犹豫地想要给他介绍一个重庆女孩来相亲。这可把有些内敛的Chris弄得面红耳赤。不过Chris知道，当这里的人想要给他介绍一个女孩认识时，表示她们认可他的人品。

在“姥姥家”的第一天，Chris沉浸在这座大大的院落的历史与美之中。大姐们告诉Chris，这个院子有一百多年的历史了，是清朝时候就修建好的，代表着中国北方传

统的乡村绅士的居住方式。院子外围是不规则的石头垒成的墙，缝隙中抹的是泥土。石墙上爬满爬山虎，在夏天的阳光中显得翠绿可爱，莹莹生光。院子里是用砖砌成的房屋，四四方方。房屋的门窗全都是用木头做的，窗棂上是传统的中国纹饰。Chris在北京的颐和园、故宫都看到过类似的纹饰，不过这里的更加简单、质朴。对Chris来说，这样古朴干净的房屋让人有一种亲切感。走进屋子，屋内全是现代的简约设计和便捷齐全的生活设施。这种古老和现代的艺术结合，让Chris在中国的乡村中寻找到了既遥远神秘又亲切贴心的美的感觉。

在"姥姥家"的第二天，Chris很早就跟着大姐们一起去田地里采摘蔬菜。当他走到田地时，他发现当地人已经挑着担子、弯着腰开始了一天的劳作。中国人是勤劳的，无论是在忙碌的大城市还是在这个偏远安静的小乡村，他们都早早地出来工作。Chris从低矮的辣椒苗的顶端摘下红红绿绿的小辣椒，从用树枝搭建的高高的架子上摘下垂得长长的豇豆。当大姐们手里抱着摘下来的黄瓜时，Chris赶紧帮忙把黄瓜小心翼翼地放到竹筐里。这些蔬菜都那么娇嫩而新鲜，充满着大自然的气息。采摘结束后，Chris抓到一只天牛。在这里，到处都能发现田园的乐趣。而田园更大的乐趣是在劳作一番后，大姐们用这刚采摘下的食材做成了一道道美味的素食：嚼劲十足的手擀面，浓郁的茄子卤让人垂涎三尺；乡村煎豆腐表面色泽金黄、酥脆，一口咬下去饱满多汁；麻辣杏鲍菇让喜欢川菜的Chris完全停不下筷子。吃完由自己采摘的食物做成的饭菜后，Chris感慨道："这趟旅行使我大开眼界。"中国的乡村田园是安静的、富足的，也是充满了历史记忆和现代感的。

在“姥姥家”的第三天，Chris 亲手准备了一道来自英国乡村的美食——南瓜浓汤。在他看来，来自英国的田园美食和中国的乡村田园可以搭配得很好。因为只有最新鲜的南瓜才能做出最美味的南瓜浓汤，而在中国的乡村，这些食材都是如此的新鲜。Chris 熟练地做好南瓜浓汤后，又充满仪式感地将浓汤盛入每一个被掏空了的小南瓜里——这是一种天然的食物容器。当他带着满脸幸福的笑容端着南瓜浓汤走进餐厅时，大姐们和当地的朋友已经静静地坐在桌前等候他了。他们在送别 Chris 之前决定要一起

聚餐。餐桌上除了Chris的南瓜浓汤，就只有中国传统的手擀面条。食物非常的简单质朴，却充满了彼此深厚的情谊。英国的南瓜浓汤和中国的手擀面条，这两道最简单的食物成为Chris与当地人交流的方式。吃面条的时候，大家纷纷笑着展示自己使用筷子的本事。这让Chris再一次感受到农家生活的质朴、欢乐。

在中国农家的三日时光很快就过去了。当Chris向大家道别时，大姐们塞给了Chris自家种的西红柿、茄子、玉米、南瓜等食材。她们知道，Chris和她们一样都喜欢这样的乡村和乡村生长的食材。正如Chris自己说的那样："虽然我们说着不同的语言，有着不同的文化背景，但是对食物和生活中酸甜苦辣的体验是一样的。"中国田园生活的简单、质朴和乐趣与外国田园生活一般无二，在田园里生活的人都珍惜和享受着土地最慷慨的馈赠。

Scan for a Video

编辑部里的“洋女婿”

“Foreign Son-in-Law” in the English Editorial Department

"Foreign Son-in-Law" in the English Editorial Department

It is a busy work day morning. The compound of the China Foreign Languages Publishing Administration on Baiwanzhuang Street in Beijing's Xicheng District is bathed in the morning sunshine. Before the work day is to begin, a foreigner with a high nose and deep eyes dressed in plain clothing hurries into a small office. After putting down his bag, he makes a cup of tea and turns on his computer. He retrieves the file which he didn't finish revising yesterday, and begins tapping skillfully on the keyboard, starting his day's work. He is David Ferguson, a senior editorial expert of the English Editorial Department of the Foreign Languages Publishing House.

Mr. Ferguson is from Scotland. Those who meet him for the first time probably consider him a gentle and simple person, and would probably find it difficult to understand just how rich and exciting his life has been. He was a top student who obtained his bachelor's degree in law in the late 1970s. He got 710 points on his GMAT test in the early

1990s. He is proficient in French, German and Italian. He has worked and lived in more than 30 countries and has a wealth of experience gained from many jobs. He has worked as a management consultant, operated a media company, and has been a writer, journalist, editor and translator. While serving as a media production manager, Mr. Ferguson got acquainted with many celebrities such as former England well-known football player David Beckham, former Manchester United coach Sir Alex Ferguson and many others, and has forged friendships with them. In 2004, he gained a new identity as a Chinese son-in-law, and his love for China began.

In 2006, he followed his wife to China. In 2008, because of many years of his experience in the media, he was employed as a journalist for china.com.cn (china.org.cn) under the China Foreign Languages Publishing Administration, and began to observe and report on China from his own perspective. Not long after he started working, an earthquake occurred in Wenchuan in western China's Sichuan Province. Ferguson's first important job was to go to Sichuan to report on the earthquake and the post-disaster relief work. He was shocked to see the great loss caused to the local people and the pain experienced by them, but was impressed by their bravery and resilience in rebuilding their homes after the disaster. After that experience, he reported on a series of major events such as the Beijing Olympic Games and the Shanghai World Expo, and gained a deep understanding of the friendly exchanges between China and the rest of the world. In early 2010, he started a new career as an English editorial expert at the Foreign Languages Publishing House. This job requires not only a high level of language proficiency but also a broad international vision and objective and fair values. Ferguson says that he likes his new job very much and puts a lot of energy into improving his revisions. He also spends time chatting with colleagues about work and reads professional books. He worked on editing the English versions of a series of Chinese government white papers and also the English versions of the first and second volumes of *Xi Jinping: The Governance of China*. Many books published by the Foreign Languages Publishing House are about China's national policies and social system. The biggest problem Ferguson encountered in his work was how to accurately and faithfully translate the essence of President Xi Jinping's speeches. "We needed to consider Western cultures and languages while doing translation," he says. Ferguson and his colleagues held meetings every morning to discuss the translation of relevant English words to make the English version as close as possible to the original meaning. With this spirit of diligence and responsibility, Ferguson and his colleagues have completed the English translations and revisions of a series of important books. In addition to his work at the Foreign Languages Publishing House, Ferguson also teaches at the Beijing International Studies University. He is liked by his students because of his patience and teaching methods.

After having lived in China for many years, Ferguson is impressed by the tremendous changes that have taken place in Chinese society since the implementation of the country's reform and opening-up policy. He says that it is remarkable. Countless Chinese people have been lifted out of poverty because of the policy, with their living standards greatly improved. "I think probably the most important area of reform from my perspective in terms of China and the world is poverty alleviation... In the past few years, China has made world-renowned achievements in poverty alleviation. No one can deny these great achievements. The rest of the world can learn from China's experience in this area." Ferguson also has his own views on the friendly cooperation between China and the rest of the world. "The Belt and Road Initiative is significant to the entire world in that it is helping change the future prospects of many developing countries which will help reshape world power." As a foreigner who has worked in the media and has lived in China for many years, Ferguson believes that many reports by some Western media have been biased against China. Many authors of these reports have not even been to China, let alone know about

China. Such so-called reports are not authentic and objective at all and mislead the people in their countries. Some countries are unwilling to see the rise of China and continue spreading "China threat" and "China expansion" fallacies, deliberately tarnishing China's image. Media in China should firmly refute these fallacies so that the world can see the real China. "As an English language editorial expert, I should continue to promote communication and ensure that China is truly understood by other countries."

While speaking of China's reform and opening up, Ferguson recalls the story of his first trip to his wife's hometown in the city of Jilin in northeast China's Jilin Province. In 2006, he accompanied his wife to return to her parents' home in Jilin for the first time. At that time, the residential buildings in Jilin seemed old and dusty, and buildings such as hospitals, schools and fitness centers were also inadequate. In Ferguson's view, people seemed to be living a very monotonous life, simply going to work and returning home every day. They stayed there for some time, and Ferguson found it difficult to adapt, and he began to miss his hometown in Scotland. He could not find a bar in Jilin to have a drink to relieve his homesickness, which was a little unbearable for him. Moreover, he had not seen any other Westerners in the city. Although his wife's family treated him very kindly, he still felt lonely. When he returned to the city more than ten years later, he found that the city had undergone earth-shattering changes: the old and dilapidated residential buildings were replaced by modern high-rises; there were more modern schools and hospitals than before, and stadiums, libraries, and thriving commercial streets had been constructed. These improvements helped make people's lives more fulfilling. There were also new wide and flat expressways and main urban roads, helping facilitate urban development. But what made him most happy was seeing more foreigners living in Jilin, many of whom were overseas students and business people. These changes have helped Ferguson see the true, rapid changes in the process of China's reform and opening up. They are also evidence of the increasingly frequent exchanges between China and the rest of the world.

Ferguson has lived in China for many years, and says that he deeply loves this country and its people. He likes to exercise every morning in the beautiful Purple Bamboo Park, and will sing Beijing Opera when he feels like it. He enjoys riding the shared bikes through the streets and hutongs of Beijing, and meeting together in a bustling bar with Chinese and foreign friends to drink and chat about work and life and feel the blend and differences of Chinese and Western cultures. Over these years, as a Chinese "foreign son-in-law", Ferguson has witnessed the changes in China and has also felt the Chinese people's yearning for a better life. He says that he is very happy living in China. "Many people want me to tell them more about China, and I am happy to tell them all about China's current development. I hope that I can help more foreigners understand the real China."

编辑部里的“洋女婿”

工作日的早晨总是紧张忙碌的。位于北京市西城区百万庄大街的中国外文局大院沐浴在晨光中。虽然离上班时间还有一会儿，但一位高鼻梁、深眼窝、衣着朴素的外国人已经匆匆地走进了一间小小的办公室。放下包，他先为自己泡上一杯清茶，接着打开电脑，调出昨天没有看完的稿件，手指轻快地敲击着键盘，开始了一天的工作。他就是外文出版社英文部的资深改稿专家——大卫·弗格森（David Ferguson）。

弗格森先生来自英国。第一次跟他接触

的人都会觉得他是一个性格温和、平实的人，无论是从外表还是言谈举止上看，人们都很难想象到他的人生经历有多么丰富、精彩：他是高材生——20世纪70年代末获得法学学士学位，90年代初GMAT考试成绩拿到710分，精通法语、德语、意大利语；他是阅历丰富的职场多面手，曾先后在30多个国家工作和生活，做过管理顾问，开过传媒公司，还是作家、记者、编辑和翻译。在担任媒体制作经理时，弗格森先生结识了很多名人，如前英格兰国脚大卫·贝克汉姆、前曼联队主教练亚历克斯·弗格森爵士，等等，并与他们结下了友谊。2004年，他多了一个新身份——中国女婿，一段与中国的情缘也就此开始了。

2006年，弗格森跟随自己的妻子来到中国发展。2008年，他凭借自己多年的媒体工作经验，应聘成为中国外文局旗下的中国网的记者，开始用自己的视角观察和报道发展中的中国。工作开始没多久，中国四川的汶川地区就发生了地震，弗格森到中国网的第一个重要工作就是南下报道汶川地震的灾情和灾后救援工作。地震给当地人民造成的巨大损失和伤痛，以及中国人民灾后重建家园的勇敢、坚强给弗格森留下了非常深刻的印象，让他感动不已。在这之后，他又相继参与了北京奥运会、上海世博会等一系列重大事件的报道，对中国与世界各国的友好交流活动有了深入的了解。2010 年初，弗格森开始了一段新的工作历程，成为外文出版社的英文改稿专家。这项工作不仅对语言水平要求很高，而且也要求工作者有广阔的国际视野和客观公正的价值观。弗格森很喜欢自己的新工作。为提高改稿水平他付出了很多精力，与同事聊业务、翻阅专业书籍、总结经验心得……很快，他就能把新工作做得有

声有色了。其间，他参与了一系列中国政府白皮书的英文改稿，还参与了《习近平谈治国理政》第一、二卷英文版的改稿工作。外文社出版的对外图书中，有很多是关于中国的国家政策和社会制度的。弗格森在工作中碰到的最大问题就是如何准确传神地翻译习近平主席讲话的精髓。"我们在翻译的时候需要考虑西方人的文化和语言习惯。"为做好重点词汇的翻译工作，弗格森和他的同事们每天早上都会准时开个小会，研讨相关词汇的译法，争取使翻译的文稿能够贴近外国读者的阅读习惯。秉持着这种认真负责的精神，弗格森和同事们一起完成了一系列重要书稿的英文翻译和改稿工作。在外文社的工作之外，弗格森还担任着北京第二外国语学院的教学工作。他对学生非常耐心，课上得很精彩，因此也受到了同学们的欢迎。

在中国生活了这么多年，弗格森对中国改革开放以来发生的巨大变化深有感触。他觉得中国的改革开放非常了不起，无数中国人因为改革开放而摆脱了贫困，生活水平获得了明显的提升。弗格森评价说："在我看来，

中国在改革方面为自己乃至为世界带来的最大的变化就是扶贫……这几年来，中国在扶贫方面取得了举世瞩目的成就，在减贫方面做出的伟大成绩没有人可以否定，世界上其他国家都应该来学习中国的扶贫经验。”对于中国与世界各国的友好共建，弗格森也有自己的见解：“‘一带一路’倡议具有国际意义，它改变了许多落后国家和发展中国家的未来前景，推动了世界力量的重塑。”作为一个在中国生活了很多年的外国人、一个媒体工作者，弗格森认为，西方的一些媒体对中国的很多报道存在偏见，不少报道文章的作者甚至都没有来过中国，更谈不上对中国有多么了解，这样的所谓“报道”根本没有真实性和客观性，会误导本国民众。有些国家不愿意看到中国崛起，不停地提中国威胁论、中国扩张论，故意抹黑中国形象，中国的对外宣传工作应该对这些国家进行有力的驳斥，让世界看到真实的中国。他说："作为改稿人，我们更应该继续加强传播，并确保中国真正地被其他国家所理解。"

说起改革开放，弗格森特别愿意回忆他第一次去妻子的家乡吉林的故事——2006年，他陪着妻子回娘家，第一次踏上了吉林的黑土地。那时的吉林，住宅楼都很老旧、灰扑扑的，医院、学校和健身场所等城市的基础设施也都不健全，人们每天就是上班、回家，生活得很传统，在弗格森看来也很单调。在吉林待了一段时间后，弗格森感觉很难适应，尤其是当他想念家乡苏格兰时，这么大的一座城市却连个可以喝上一杯以解乡愁的酒吧都没有，这让他有点儿受不了。而且，他在吉林生活的那段时间里没有见过其他西方人，虽然妻子的家人对他都非常亲切，可是弗格森还是感到了孤独。而十多年后，当他再次回到吉林的时候，他发现这座城市发生了翻天覆地的变化：老旧破败的住宅楼被现代化的高楼大厦取代，学校和医院比原来多了，而且建设得更加现代化，体育场、图书馆和繁华的商业街让人们的生活更充实，宽阔平坦的环城高速和城市主干道提升了城市发展的效率……最让他感到开心的是，在吉林居住的外国人也明显多了起来，他们中有很多人是在中国上学的留学生和做生意的商人。这些变化让弗格森真真切切地体会到了中国社会改革开放进程中日新月异的变化，也让他看到了中国与世界的交往越来越频繁。

在中国生活了这么多年，弗格森觉得自己已经深深地爱上了这个国家和这里的人们。他喜欢每天清晨到美丽的紫竹院公园锻炼身体，高兴了还会放开嗓子唱一段京剧；他喜欢骑着方便的共享单车绿色出行，游遍北京的大街小巷；他更喜欢在热闹的酒吧里和中外好友共聚一堂，喝喝小酒聊聊工作和生活，感受中西方文化的交融与碰撞。这些年，弗格森作为一名中国的“洋女婿”，见证了中国方方面面的变化，也感受到了中国人民对于美好生活的向往和努力追求。他觉得自己生活在中国很幸福，他说："许多人找我了解中国的情况，我会积极地向他们介绍中国发展的现状，希望更多的外国人能够通过我了解一个真正的中国！"

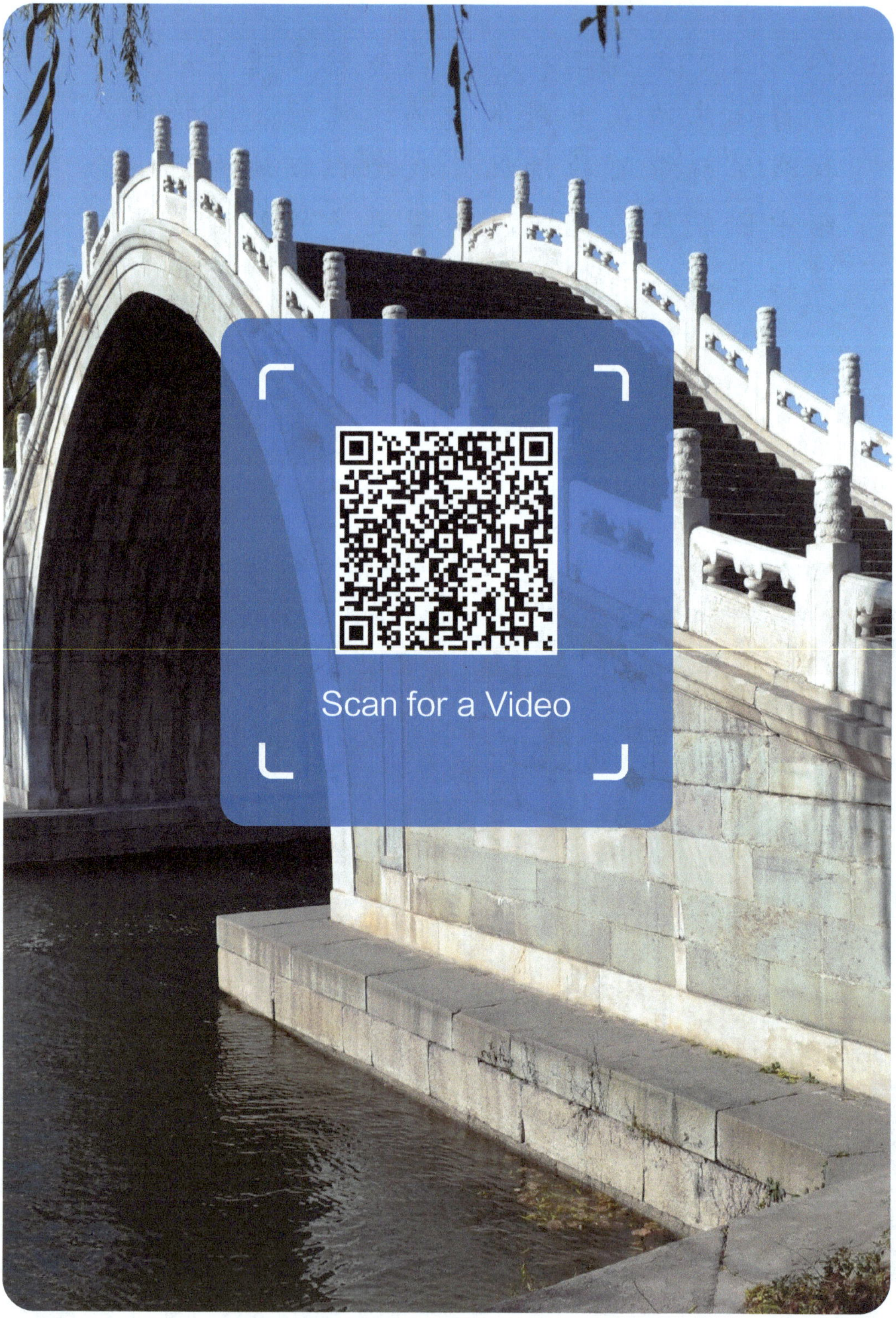
Scan for a Video

坦桑尼亚的配音演员

A Tanzanian Dubbing Actress in China

A Tanzanian Dubbing Actress in China

In the southeastern suburbs of Beijing at the dubbing studio of the StarTimes Group Headquarters, dubbing actress Hilder Edimund Malecela from Tanzania is closely watching a large TV screen as she dubs a Chinese TV show in Swahili.

Hilder grew up in the countryside near Dar es Salaam, Tanzania. When she was a college student, she saw a film starring Jackie Chan. Deeply impressed by the Chinese kung fu in the film, she made up her mind to work in the film and TV industry in the future. After graduation, she became a professional dubbing voice-over actress.

In 2011, the Chinese TV series *Beautiful Daughter-in-Law* became a hit in Tanzania. Again, Hilder was moved by the Chinese story. She became obsessed with the plot. She says, "In addition to kung fu, I found China's long-standing culture and modern cities also so fascinating."

"Many Tanzanians like to watch Chinese TV shows, films, and documentaries," Hilder says. "They talk a lot about China. Compared with Tanzania, China is much more developed." She goes on to say, "I bet you didn't know that dubbed Chinese TV shows are very famous in Tanzania. Many people like them very much, and they especially love the plot of *Beautiful Daughter-in-Law*. We've dubbed a lot of shows and Tanzanians like them because they learn a lot." Despite the cultural differences, there are many similarities between the two countries, such as the relationship between a mother-in-law and a daughter-in-law, and conflicts among family members. That's why *Beautiful Daughter-in-Law* evokes a strong emotional response among the Tanzanian audience. The common themes of marriage and family transcend the culture gap as Tanzanians watch the show, which portrays the pursuit of a happy life by an ordinary Chinese family, a pursuit which is common among all cultures. Subsequently, a large number of Chinese films and TV shows have become popular in Tanzania, such as *Mother's Glorious Days*, *The Wishes of an Old Daddy*, and *The Happy Life of Jin Tailang*.

As a fan of Chinese culture, Hilder also likes to participate in Chinese festival celebrations. She also loves watching Chinese dancing, and in her free time she often dances, which also helps her learn more about Chinese culture.

"I came to China in 2015, but only stayed for four months. But I've been working at StarTimes now for almost two years." In 2016, The First StarTimes Cup Chinese TV Series and Films Swahili Dubbing Competition was held in Tanzania. Hilder immediately signed up for the initial audition and took first place with her excellent performance,

which won her a position as a dubbing actress at the Chinese company StarTimes Group. Since then, she has become somewhat of a messenger of Chinese-African cultural exchange.

In 2017, Hilder attended the "Thematic Session on People-to-People Connectivity at the Belt and Road Forum for International Cooperation." During the forum, she and her partners showed an excerpt of *Journey to the West* dubbed in Swahili, which won high praise of the audience. "Sharing is the key to interpersonal connectivity," she says. "These TV series and films have shortened the distance between us, turning the 10,000-km distance into face-to-face contact."

The friendship between China and Tanzania has a long history. As early as the 1960s, Chinese workers in Tanzania helped build the Tanzania-Zambia Railway. There is also the Ubungo Flyover Project in Dar es Salaam, a three-tiered flyover with ramps currently under construction to help ease traffic congestion in the busy city. It is the first flyover project launched by the Tanzanian government, and is being built by the East African Branch of the China Civil Engineering Construction Corporation. Launched in March 2017, eighty percent of the project has been completed, and it is expected to open to traffic in 2020. Hilder says, "The Chinese government and its people have been contributing a lot to my homeland. As we all know, there are no flyovers in Tanzania. The Chinese people are helping our government build one, and the project is still under construction."

Hilder is not only an outstanding dubbing actress, but she is also adept at translation work and using related software and equipment. "As a dubbing actress, my role should be focused on helping Tanzanians better understand Chinese culture. I also do translation work, translating Chinese films into my native language. I often use the simple language so that all Tanzanians can understand easily so that we can attract our audience and help them understand Chinese culture."

In February 2018, Hilder returned to Tanzania for a vacation. In Dar es Salaam, she gave lessons on dubbing to a local women's art troupe. She taught them about the importance of dubbing with emotion and conveying the right mood, as well as other dubbing and translation skills. She also imparted some positive life lessons she had learned while working in China. She encouraged them to tap into their potential and not be afraid to work outside their hometowns, and also to realize their value in society.

"I hope that through my life experiences more Africans will come to like Chinese culture and that I can help them broaden their horizons and keep pace with the times," she says. "I hope to continue my dubbing job in China, and when my child grows up, I want him to come to study in China."

Thanks to the Belt and Road Initiative, there have been more business and trade contacts between China and Tanzania, and an increasing number of Chinese enterprises have established companies and factories in Tanzania. The Chinese language is also gaining popularity in Tanzania as it can be used in everyday life and study. Every year, Chinese teachers and students come to conduct exchanges and study in Tanzania, offering teaching assistance to local schools. Many young Tanzanians like Hilder are learning Chinese and hope to study and work in China in the future.

"I will work even harder to set a good example for more Tanzanians," she says. To enable more Tanzanians to better understand Chinese culture, she works hard every day to improve her dubbing quality. "Only through attractive films and TV shows can I help more Tanzanians appreciate Chinese culture."

坦桑尼亚的配音演员

在位于北京亦庄的四达时代集团总部配音工作室里，来自坦桑尼亚的配音演员希尔德（Hilder Edimund Malecela）紧盯屏幕，正用斯瓦希里语声情并茂地给中国影视剧配音。

希尔德从小生活在坦桑尼亚达累斯萨拉姆的农村。她在上大学的时候，一个偶然的机会看到了成龙主演的电影。电影中经典的中国功夫令希尔德印象深刻，她从此立志，希望今后能够从事影视剧方面的工作。毕业后，希尔德成为一名专业配音演员。

2011年，中国电视剧《媳妇的美好时代》在坦桑尼亚热播。希尔德再一次近距离“接触”中国，她被影片中的故事深深吸引。“除了中国功夫，中国悠久的文化和现代化的都市也令人如此着迷。”希尔德说。

“在坦桑尼亚，很多人都喜欢看中国电视剧和电影，还有中国的纪录片，坦桑人经常谈论中国，经常把中国挂在嘴上。跟坦桑尼亚相比，中国要发达很多。”希尔德说，“你知道吗，中国的配音剧在坦桑尼亚很有名。很多人都非常喜欢这些剧。很多人也非常喜欢《媳妇的美好时代》这部剧的剧情。我们配了很多剧，观众也很喜欢，我忘了叫什么名字……但是都是坦桑观众喜欢的剧，他们从剧中也学到了很多东西。”虽然中坦两国有文化上的差异，但婆媳之间的关系、家人之间的矛盾有很大的共通性，因此《媳妇的美好时代》引起了观众们的强烈共鸣。婚姻与家庭这个共同话题使坦桑尼亚观众跨越了文化差异，通过感受一家普通人的喜怒哀乐体验到了对美好生活的追求。而这种追求在不同的文化之间都是相通的。此后，一大批中国影视剧陆续登上坦桑尼亚的荧幕。《妈妈的花样年华》《老爸的心愿》《金太郎的幸福生活》等电视剧都深受坦桑尼亚观众的喜爱。

作为一个热爱中国文化的坦桑尼亚人，希尔德每到过节的时候总会参加一些中国人组织的活动，她非常喜欢看人跳舞，尤其欣赏中国舞蹈，在闲暇时间她也会参与其中，

通过舞蹈了解更多的中国文化。

“我在2015年来过中国，那时候我只待了4个月，但这次我来四达工作已经快两年了。”希尔德说。2016年，“首届四达杯中国影视剧斯瓦希里语配音大赛”在坦桑尼亚举办。希尔德第一时间就去报名参加了海选，凭借优异的表现获得第一名。通过配音大赛，希尔德获得了在中国企业四达时代集团的配音工作，也从此成为一名中非文化交流的使者。

2017年，希尔德参加了“一带一路”国际合作高峰论坛“增进民心相通”平行主题会议。会上，希尔德和她的小伙伴们为大

家带来了斯瓦西里语配音的《西游记》节选，赢得了观众的一致好评。“民心相通最重要的是分享。”希尔德说，“影视作品的传播拉近了我们的距离，让1万公里的航程变成了面对面。”

中国和坦桑尼亚的友谊源远流长，早在20世纪60年代，中国人民就帮助这个非洲朋友修建了著名的坦赞铁路。乌本戈立交桥是坦桑尼亚政府主导的第一个立交桥项目，主要由一座三层立交桥和配套分流道路构成，由中土集团东非有限公司承建。该项目于2017年3月奠基，目前施工进度已接近80%，预计2020年内竣工通车。“在我们国家，中国政府和人民帮我们做了很多事，而且直到现在还在继续。你知道吗？立交桥，坦桑尼亚到现在还没有。中国人民帮助我们的政府建造了一座，它现在还在建设中。”希尔德说。

在配音工作的岗位上，希尔德不仅是一名优秀的配音演员，还能胜任翻译工作，熟练使用相关软件设备。“作为一个配音演员，我的作用应该是让更多的坦桑尼亚观众了解中国文化。我同时在这里也做翻译工作，将中国电影翻译成我们当地的语言。我会用最简单的语言让所有坦桑尼亚人都能明白，这样我们就能更好地抓住观众，让他们明白中国文化。”希尔德说。

2018年2月，休假回国的希尔德在达

累斯萨拉姆给当地一个女性艺术团讲起了配音课，向她们传授配音情绪、配音和翻译技巧等方面的知识。课堂上，她还把在中国工作中领悟到的一些积极的人生态度带给当地女性，鼓励她们发挥自己的能力外出工作，实现自己的社会价值。

“我希望通过自己的人生经历和经验让更多非洲的朋友喜欢上中国文化，更希望帮助他们打开眼界，跟上时代变化。”希尔德说，“我希望能继续待在中国，把配音工作一直干下去，等孩子长大了，也想让他来中国读书。”

在“一带一路”的积极作用下，中国和坦桑尼亚的商贸往来日益密切，越来越多的

中国企业在坦桑尼亚建立公司，开办工厂。汉语已经在坦桑尼亚广泛传播，生活、学习等越来越多的方面都少不了汉语。如今，每年都有中国的老师和学生到坦桑尼亚交流学习，为当地的学校提供教学帮助，也有越来越多像希尔德一样的年轻人在学习中文，希望到中国来求学、工作。

“我要更加努力工作，通过自身的示范，让更多以我为榜样的人从中受益。”希尔德说。为了能让更多的坦桑尼亚人了解中国文化，她每天都在努力工作，提高自己作品的质量，她说：“只有作品抓住观众，才能够让更多的人了解中国文化。”

Scan for a Video

陶益壮的中国科研梦

A Frenchman's Scientific Research Dream in China

A Frenchman's Scientific Research Dream in China

In a Xi'an Jiaotong University laboratory, the "droplet collision" experiment is well under way. Professor Marie-Jean Thoraval is the lead researcher in charge of the experiment. After numerous tests, a smile finally forms on his face.

Born in 1984, Professor Marie-Jean Thoraval is originally from France. He came to the School of Aerospace at Xi'an Jiaotong University in Shaanxi, China in September 2015 to engage in scientific research and teaching. His Chinese name is Tao Yizhuang. His primary field of study is fluid mechanics, specifically the study of droplet and bubble dynamics, a field which he believes could produce miracles at any moment.

The origin of Professor Thoraval's interest in Chinese culture can be traced back to high school in France where he took Chinese as an

elective language course. He said that he met an outstanding Chinese teacher who taught him with great patience. He had thought of coming to China ever since. In October 2006, he was selected as one of the 100 young French scientists to visit China. Along with then French President Jacques René Chirac, the delegation visited many universities and companies in Beijing, Wuhan and Shanghai. Upon graduation as a postgraduate student, he applied for internship at the French Embassy in China and worked as an aviation analyst there. The six-month internship made him realize that only through acquiring more professional knowledge could he get more opportunities in the fast-growing Chinese economy. At that time, he'd already made up his mind to stay in China.

In 2013, he received his PhD in engineering from the King Abdullah University of Science & Technology in Saudi Arabia. From 2013 to 2015, he worked with the Physics of Fluids Team at the University of Twente in the Netherlands to conduct further post-doctoral research. On one occasion, a fellow researcher told him about an International Center of Applied Mechanics at Xi'an Jiaotong University in China, a key national laboratory. He was keenly aware that the laboratory was better equipped to suit his specific field of research, so he decided to go to China to apply for a post at the university. In 2015, he was hired by the university as a distinguished research fellow, focusing on interfacial flows of fluid mechanics and droplet and bubble dynamics. In 2016, he was admitted into the National Thousand Young Talents Program and became a doctoral supervisor. In 2017, he won the honorary title of "Outstanding Overseas Teacher of Shaanxi Province" and was shortlisted for the third "Top Ten New Academic Researchers" and also for the first group of "Zhongying Young Scholars of Xi'an Jiaotong University." After building a platform, organizing a new team, and recruiting students, he formed his own scientific research path in China.

In Professor Thoraval's view, China is a fast-developing country which has many opportunities and is providing great support to scientific research. During his first trip to China, he witnessed the tremendous changes brought about by the fast-growing economy. He saw the great development and changes in Xi'an, an ancient city with a long history and rich culture. He thinks that Xi'an is an old but modern city, with convenient transportation which makes it very easy for him to travel to other Chinese cities or even go to France or other countries. "After coming to Xi'an, I find that it is a historical and cultural city, which is fast-developing. The subways are built quickly and very convenient. My hometown is in the French Alps, so I love climbing mountains around Xi'an where the scenery is so amazing." He also likes Xi'an cuisine, especially noodles. He and his wife and child have settled down in the city.

He gets very excited when talking about fluid mechanics. "Here I can use a high-speed camera which can capture 2.1 million frames per second to see a world we could never see with our own eyes. Such video helps us discover many new things in scientific research." The high-speed camera plays a key role in the field of fluid mechanics as it can capture the dynamics phenomena of droplets and bubbles. Having the advanced high-speed photographic system in the laboratory is actually a prerequisite for carrying out such research. In 2020, Professor Thoraval and his team made great progress in the research of the rebound of self-lubricating compound drops, which is a typical example of basic research to lay the foundation for more sophisticated research on precise and complex droplet sedimentation which has a significant influence on 2D and 3D printing and droplet separation/oil-water separation. It's also worth mentioning that one of the team's photographic works won the Photron Company's Best Science Award in 2018. "China is a country that respects scientific development, and the Chinese government has offered great policy-related support and favorable conditions for my research work. In 2016, I was selected to become a member of the National Thousand Young Talents Program, was promoted to Class A of the 'Youth Talent Support Program' of the university, and became a doctoral supervisor. All this encourages me to continue devoting myself to my scientific research and experiments. I am getting much closer to realizing my dream," he says. To facilitate his research, he presided over the construction of a 70-m^2 laboratory with constant temperature and humidity in strict accordance with international standards, well-equipped with chemical preparation equipment and other apparatus to observe fluid mechanics. In early 2017, the laboratory was completed, which marked the beginning of new research on droplet and bubble dynamics at Xi'an Jiaotong University. But as more progress has been made in the field of fluid

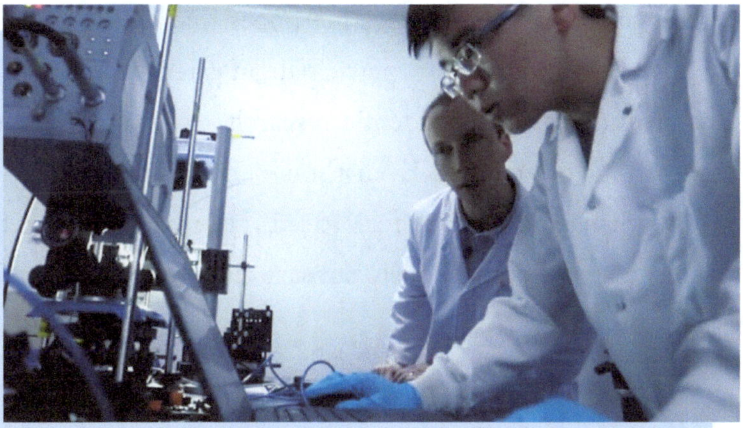

mechanics, the size of the new laboratory currently cannot meet their daily research requirements. The construction of the Innovation Harbor Fluid Mechanics Platform will provide him with a new opportunity. Professor Thoraval is eager to move to a larger platform as soon as possible to carry out new research. The installation of the Innovation Harbor Fluid Mechanics Platform at the university is basically completed, and he hopes that in the future the Innovation Harbor Fluid Mechanics Platform can give him more opportunities to promote interdisciplinary research and cooperation.

"Scientific research has always been my dream. In the future, I want to turn my laboratory into an international top-notch research platform, and I hope my team can make more contributions to China's development." Professor Thoraval has published several papers in international journals in the field of fluid mechanics such as *Physical Review Letters*, *Science Advances* and *Physics of Fluids*. He is the supervisor of 13 students (three PhD and ten Master's Degree candidates), and also teaches weekly lessons to postgraduate students. He provides each student with a tailor-made study plan. In addition to the weekly meeting, he also offers research tutoring, academic reports and lectures on important subjects. He hopes that all his students can lay a solid academic foundation, participate in extensive research, adopt a serious attitude towards academic research, and be meticulous and passionate about their work. Even though he is under such a high-intensity work pace, he never feels tired. He is determined to lead his research team to continuously surpass themselves and realize his Chinese dream.

陶益壮的中国科研梦

在西安交通大学的实验室内，一个名为液滴碰撞的实验正在有序进行，而这场实验的指挥官陶益壮（Marie-Jean Thoraval）教授经过反复试验，脸上终于露出一丝微笑。

Marie-Jean Thoraval 教授，1984 年生，法国人，2015 年 9 月份来到中国西安交通大学航天航空学院从事科研教学工作，他还给自己取了个中文名字——陶益壮。他的主要研究方向为流体力学领域中的液滴和气泡动力学，他认为这是一个随时都能产生奇迹的领域。

陶益壮教授对中国文化兴趣的萌芽可以追溯到他的高中时期，当时的他在许多可以选修的外语中选择了中文。陶益壮说，那时自己遇到了一位非常棒的中文老师，特别耐心地教他学习中文。由此，他便产生了来到中国的想法。2006年10月，他被选为访问中国的法国百名青年科学家之一，同法国前总统希拉克一同访问了北京、武汉及上海的多个大学和公司。硕士毕业之后，他抓住了到法国驻中国大使馆实习的机会，任法国驻中国大使馆航空分析师。通过6个月的航空分析师实习，他深刻地体会到只有掌握更强的专业知识才能够在中国快速的经济发展中获得更多的机会。此时的他已在心中种下了

在中国扎根的种子。

2013年，陶益壮在沙特阿拉伯阿卜杜拉国王科技大学获得工学博士学位。2013年至2015年，他在荷兰屯特大学Physics of Fluids团队读博士后。一次偶然的机会，陶益壮的同学告诉他，在中国西安交通大学有个国际应用力学中心，也是国家级重点实验室。陶益壮深知这样的实验室可以为自己提供更广阔的研究平台，于是他毅然来到西安交通大学应聘。终于，2015年他被西安交通大学聘为特聘研究员，以流体力学中的界面流体领域为方向，重点对液滴和气泡动力学进行研究。2016年，他成功入选国家青年千人计划，获得博士生导师资格。2017年，他又接连获得陕西省优秀外籍教师荣誉称号，并入围学校第三届“十大学术新人”和首批“仲英青年学者”。搭建平台、组建团队、招收学生，就这样，陶益壮在中国开启了自己的科研之路。

在陶益壮看来，中国是一个发展很快的国家，而且有着更多的机会，对科研的扶持力度也很大。第一次来到中国他就目睹了中国经济快速发展带来的翻天覆地的变化。来到西安以后，他更是看到了西安这座历史文化古城的发展和变迁。他觉得西安是一座古老又现代的城市，这里交通便利，无论去中国的其他城市还是去国外，抑或回法国都十分便捷。“我来了西安以后，我感觉西安是一个有文化有历史的城市，也是一个发展很快的城市。地铁建得很快，很方便。我的老家在阿尔卑斯山，所以我特别喜欢在西安附近爬山，风景也特别漂亮。”陶益壮说。他也很喜欢西安的美食，面条是他的最爱。现

在，陶益壮和妻子、孩子已经定居西安。

说到流体力学，陶益壮便兴奋起来，“在这里我可以使用每秒 210 万张照片的高速相机去看我们用自己的眼睛看不到的世界，会发现很多新的事物，可以用这个视频做一个很漂亮的研究结果。”在流体力学领域中，高速摄像机十分重要，可以捕捉液滴和气泡的动力学现象，实验室中先进的高速摄影系统是多项研究得以顺利开展的前提。2020 年，陶益壮团队进行的自润滑液滴反弹研究取得新进展。该研究是基础科学研究的一个典型，为精密复杂液滴沉积的研究奠定了基础，对 2D、3D 打印及液滴分离/油水分离技术产生了巨大影响。另外值得一提的是，本次研究中的一份摄影作品还获得了 2018 年度 Photron 公司的最佳科学奖。“中国是一个尊重科学发展的国家，中国政府在政策方面很支持我的科研工作，给我提供了很多便利条件。2016 年，我获选国家青年千人计划，并晋升为学校‘青年拔尖人才支持计划’A 类，获得博士生导师资格，这更加激励我全身心投入到自己的科研平台和实验中，自己的科研梦想变得越来越近。”陶益壮说。为了研究，陶益壮主持建设了一个完全按照国际标准打造的70平米的恒温、恒湿洁净实验室，配备齐全的化学品制备设备及流体力学观测设备。2017年初，实验室全面竣工，预示着西安交通大学液滴和气泡动力学新研究的开始。随着学校流体力学学科的不断发展，这个不足70平米的实验空间已满足不了日常的科研需求。创新港流体力学平台的建设为此提供了契机，陶益壮表示“想要尽快搬到更大的平台去，开展更好的研究”。目前，西安交通大学空天与力学研究院流体力学平台安装已经基本到位，陶益壮期望将来到创新港流体力学平台能有更多学科交叉合作的机会。

“科学研究一直是我的梦想，未来我想把我的实验室打造成世界一流的研究平台，希望自己的团队可以为中国发展做出贡献。”陶益壮说。如今，陶益壮已在流体力学领域国际权威期刊《物理评论快报》（Physical Review Letters）、《科学》子刊《科学进展》（Science Advances）、《流体物理》

（Physics of Fluids）等期刊发表多篇论文。与此同时，他是13名研究生的导师（3名博士生，10名硕士生），每周还承担着硕士生的教学任务。他为每个学生都精心设计了培养计划，除每周例会外还包括定期的科研辅导、学术报告，以及针对重要学术问题开展的专题讲座等。他希望每个学生都能够拥有扎实的基础、广泛的涉猎、严肃的态度和无限的热情，在科学研究中一丝不苟。在如此高强度的工作节奏下，他从未觉得辛苦。陶益壮立志带领他的科研团队不断超越自我，实现他的中国梦。

Scan for a Video

北京“西城洋大爷”

“Foreign Xicheng Uncle” in Beijing

"Foreign Xicheng Uncle" in Beijing

Many people in Beijing are familiar with "Xicheng Dama", a group of smiling volunteers who are usually seen patrolling scenic spots, shopping malls, subway stations and bus stops in Xicheng District, Beijing. They usually wear their signature red vests, red armbands and red caps. "Dama" in Chinese means "aunty", and every day these warm-hearted volunteers patrol the streets and hutongs helping neighbors, passers-by, and tourists who need assistance.

In this group of volunteers, most of whom are Beijing residents, and people tend to notice the man with blue eyes, blonde hair and large nose also wearing a red vest and red armband. The passers-by are surprised to see him, but their surprise ceases after hearing his standard Beijing dialect. His participation with the volunteers adds an international touch to the group. He is Terry Crossman from the US. In the hutongs at Shichahai, people affectionately call him Xicheng Yang Daye, or "Foreign Xicheng Uncle".

Terry is 63 years old, and his Chinese name is Gao Tianrui, though his neighbors and volunteers affectionately call him Old Gao. He first came to China in 1981 on a business trip to Shanghai. At that time, he was not able to eat authentic Shanghai snacks as foreigners who came to China could only use foreign exchange certificates in places specifically designated for them, such as international restaurants and friendship stores. At that time, China just began implementing the policy of reform and opening-up, and it was slowly shifting from old to new, and from a closed society to an open one. Chinese people still used food and oil vouchers when they shopped or dined in restaurants, so foreigners also had to follow these rules. At that time, it was rare to see foreigners who could speak Chinese in Shanghai. No matter where Terry went, Chinese people would gather around him, curiously asking questions about the outside world. Terry happily told them about his experiences in the US and other countries he had visited. During his stay in Shanghai, he also witnessed the street celebrations after the Chinese women's volleyball team won the World Cup for the first time. The joyous atmosphere made him as excited as the people in Shanghai.

Terry has been living in Beijing's hutongs for more than 20 years. He likes this city and the hutong where he lives, and also his friendly and warm-hearted neighbors. He has witnessed the changing times in Beijing's hutongs. For years he has been a frequent hutong stroller. Every morning he would go out for a walk, greeting his neighbors with the idiomatic Chinese, "Have you eaten yet?" He would walk at least two kilometers through the hutongs from the Gulou (Bell Tower) to the Lotus Market. During one of his walks, he met Liu Xiaoxia, whom he affectionately calls Master Liu because it was she who coached him to become one of the volunteers.

She says that Terry found her and asked if he could become a volunteer. At first, she was doubtful. How could a foreigner who couldn't speak Chinese be a volunteer to help others? But after chatting she realized that he could speak Chinese fluently in the Beijing dialect, and that he was warm-hearted and willing to help others. In the end, he was accepted into the volunteer group. He was determined to serve the people wholeheartedly from then on.

Every day, near the Lotus Market at Shichahai, Terry helps tourists and passers-by with directions, boiled water, or public transport routes, etc. When there are many tourists, he also patrols the surrounding areas and helps maintain order. "A foreigner can speak Chinese and help us with directions!" Many Chinese tourists from other parts of the country are surprised at this. Young people jokingly call him "Foreign Uncle". "I'm a warm-hearted, optimistic and easy-going person. I like living here, and want to help others. Maybe it's fate," he says jokingly. "This is how I have become a 'Xicheng Dama'."

While talking about the changes that have taken place in Beijing over the past 20 years, Terry says impressively, "I feel that Beijing changes every day. It develops and changes with each passing day!" He says that when he had just arrived in Beijing, there were only two subway lines. But in the blink of an eye, Beijing's transportation system has spread out in all directions like a spider's web. Now it's very convenient to take public transportation wherever you want to go. You can also bind the transportation card to your mobile phone and swipe it to buy a ticket. This technology facilitates urban services. Also, there are designated bus lanes on the ring roads to enable buses to run normally and arrive on time during traffic congestion in the morning and evening rush hours.

When he first came to live in China, Terry found it hard to adapt to life here, especially the food. When he would return from visiting relatives in the United States, he would always bring several large suitcases filled with food, clothing and other things that were not available in China. But now things have changed completely. Now, specialty products from all parts of China and the world can be bought in Chinese shops, and even rare goods can be purchased through online shopping. Terry still carries large suitcases when visiting his relatives, but they are full of things "Made in China". These are gifts he brings to the United States to share with his friends.

Terry considers himself an authentic Beijinger, and not a foreigner. He likes noodles served with fried bean sauce, mutton hot pot, and various Beijing snacks. Speaking about delicious food, he says that his favorite is steamed stuffed buns dipped in vinegar. When asked why, he says it is because he has a Chinese stomach.

Wearing his red armband, Terry patrols the hutongs at Shichahai and greets passers-by with a smile. He says that living here brings him peace and happiness. Looking at the hutong where he lives, he says, "This is where I live, and where my friends live. This is my home."

北京"西城洋大爷"

提起"西城大妈"，大家可能不会陌生，北京西城区的各大景点、商场、地铁站、公交车站都能看到他们的身影和热情洋溢的笑脸。红马甲、红袖标、红帽子就是他们的标志。所谓"西城大妈"，其实就是北京西城区平安志愿者的一个代号，这个称号无关性别，而是代表着一股热心肠、助人为乐的劲头。大街小巷中，左邻右里间，每天坚持值勤、巡防的，帮助邻里、路人、游客解决各种困难的，就是这抹流动的"志愿红"。

就在这样一群充满京腔京味儿的"志愿红"中，却有一位蓝眼睛、金头发、高鼻梁，同样穿着红马甲、佩戴红袖标的老外吸引着路人的目光。他的"格格不入"让人觉得十分诧异，待到听他张口说话，一口标准的北京话却又让人恍然大悟。他的出现给"西城大妈"的群体增添了一丝"国际范儿"。来自美国的老高（Terry Crossman）在什刹海附近的胡同里溜达，周围人会亲切地称呼他为"西城洋大爷"。

“洋大爷”的中文名字叫高天瑞，今年63岁，街坊邻居和志愿者同事都亲切地称呼他为“老高”。老高第一次来中国是1981年，他在上海出差，却没办法品尝上海那些地道的小吃，让他大呼遗憾。原来，那会儿中国刚刚改革开放不久，还处在一个由旧到新、由封闭到开放的年代。老百姓出门买东西、下馆子仍然使用粮油券，而来中国的外国人则只能使用外汇券在国际饭店和友谊商店这样的专门面向外宾的地方消费。会讲汉语的老外在那个年代的上海十分稀罕，不管走到哪里都有很多人围着他，好奇地问这问那，他们都很想知道中国外面的世界是什么样子的。老高很愿意为大家讲述他在美国和他去过的其他国家的经历和见闻。在上海期间，他还见证了中国女排首次赢得世界杯后，全上海的市民在街上欢呼庆祝的场面，欢乐的

气氛也令他"入乡随俗",同样感到十分兴奋。

如今,老高已经在北京的胡同里生活了20多年,他喜欢北京,喜欢在北京的胡同生活,喜欢这里充满着人情味儿的邻里关系,他也和北京胡同一起经历着时代的变迁。老高算是一个地地道道的"胡同串子",每天早晨他都要出来遛弯儿,和街坊们逐一问好,再默契地互相问上一句"吃了吗,您"。每天早上,他从鼓楼穿过胡同走到荷花市场,至少要步行两公里。就是在那儿,老高认识了刘晓霞阿姨,老高亲切地称刘阿姨为"师父",因为正是她把老高领入了西城区平安志愿者的服务队伍。

刘阿姨说,当时老高找到她,问能不能也来当志愿者。一开始,刘阿姨心里还犯嘀咕,一个外国人,中国话都说不好,怎么能当好志愿者去服务大家。结果聊着聊着,刘阿姨发现老高的汉语说得特别顺溜,甚至还有一点儿北京口音,而且他这个人很热心肠,愿意帮助别人。就这样,老高顺利地加入了西城志愿者队伍,他对自己说,从此要一心一意为人民服务。

老高每天的工作是在什刹海荷花市场附近的岗亭为需要帮助的游客、市民解决各种各样的困难，指路、提供热水、公共交通线路引导，等等。游客多的时候，他还要去周边巡防和维持秩序。“老外会说中文，还给咱指路！”不少前来游玩的外地朋友都惊叹这是新鲜事儿，年轻人还会开玩笑地称呼他为“洋大爷”。“我就是个热心、乐观、随遇而安的人，我喜欢这里，就想和大家伙一起做点儿帮助别人的事儿，这也算是缘分吧。”老高开玩笑地说，“我就是这样变成一个西城大妈的。”

高天瑞谈起在中国生活这20多年来的变化，他不禁感叹：“我感觉北京好像每一天都不一样，北京一直在发展，日新月异！”老高说，他刚来北京的时候还只有两条地铁线，一眨眼之间北京的交通已经像张蜘蛛网一样四通八达了。现在不管去哪儿，乘坐公共交通工具都十分便捷，还可以把交通卡绑定在手机上，直接刷手机买票上车，这是科技给城市服务带来的极大便利。不仅如此，环路上还有专门的公交车道，早晚高峰遭遇堵车的时候，公交车仍然可以正常行驶，准时到达。

刚来中国生活的时候，老高觉得生活还是有一些不方便的，尤其是饮食方面。那会儿，他每次从美国探亲归来时都会带着几个大大的行李箱，里面装满了当时在中国买不到的食品、衣物和其他东西。而现在已经完全不需要了，现在的中国可以买到来自全国甚至全世界各地的特色商品，不太常见的商品也可以通过网络购物来实现。现在，老高探亲时还会带着大大的行李箱，不过里面装满了"中国制造"，这些都是他要带到美国分享给朋友们的礼物。

老高并不觉得自己是老外，他觉得自己是一个地道的北京人。他喜欢炸酱面、铜锅涮肉，还喜欢各种各样的北京小吃。谈到美食，老高说他自己最爱吃的是包子，并且一定要蘸醋。当被问到为什么喜欢吃醋的时候，他说他自己长了一个中国人的胃。

高天瑞戴着"红袖标"在什刹海的大小胡同里溜达，跟身边的路人微笑地打着招呼。生活在这里，他从心底感到安宁和喜悦。高天瑞对着自己住的胡同说："这儿是我住的地方，我朋友们的地方，这儿就是我家。"

Scan for a Video

义乌客商非洲来

An African Businessman in Yiwu

An African Businessman in Yiwu

Tirera Sourakhata, a Senegalese businessman, has been doing business in Yiwu, Zhejiang Province for 16 years. Since he has been living in China for a long time, he is used to many Chinese customs, including tea drinking. Just as Confucius said, "Isn't it a pleasure to have friends come from afar." He likes to greet his guests with tea. He sits at his tea table, following the procedures of the tea ceremony to prepare the tea and tea set. As the tea brews, the sweet fragrance emits from the pot. He says that wherever he is, he offers tea to his friends from different parts of the world because sitting and chatting while drinking tea makes people feel relaxed and comfortable. It is said that the tea ceremony embodies the Chinese way of doing business, namely no rushing and being courteous and generous to your friends. He knows this very well.

"A cup of coffee may be drunk in a minute or two, but tea tends to keep friends longer in my office. They can say what they want to.

During spontaneous conversations, they may come up with some new ideas about cooperation. Many business deals are made this way." Tirera not only speaks Chinese well, but he also understands the social customs of Chinese people.

In the early days of doing business, Tirera bought clothing from Guangzhou, which was then exported to Senegal. With the help of many Chinese partners, he changed from a novice businessman to a skillful negotiator and exporter. Although he encountered many difficulties, he made a sum of money. Two years later, on the recommendation of a friend, he came to Yiwu City. He found that the city was a hidden treasure within the trade industry with a great variety of commodities available. He then changed his main business from clothing to hardware exports. Yiwu Crestron Foreign Trade Co., Ltd. is his headquarters in China. After years of development, it has become the largest African trading company in Yiwu.

Tirera says proudly, "The business environment in Yiwu is getting better and better with high-quality and inexpensive products, highly efficient and convenient services and global logistics. Our company is developing smoothly. In 2007, it only had one employee, and now it has more than 40. Our annual turnover can amount to 4,000 to 5,000 million RMB yuan, which is something I could not have imagined over ten years ago. Yiwu's favorable economic policies are friendly to foreign business people. In return, foreign business people contribute to the vigorous development of the city. We've witnessed and have been a part of the great growth of the city."

After having learned of his thriving business, some African friends came to ask him if he could export a greater variety of goods. Now, in addition to his hardware business, he also exports over a thousand of small commodities, such as tableware, accessories, articles for everyday use, and toys to other African countries. He says, "These industrial products cannot be manufactured in Africa, so people there have to rely on imports. Yiwu products are valued by African customers because of their high quality and good price. These 'Made in China' products are popular in Africa."

Tirera says that in fact, Chinese and African cultures have a lot in common. For example, when hosting guests from afar, Chinese people always prepare a lot of dishes, even if they can't eat them up. In Senegal, a host will show his hospitality by buying and killing a sheep in front of his guest to prepare fresh mutton. The Chinese and Senegalese peoples are warm-hearted and hospitable. He has also recommended many Chinese companies to invest and set up factories in Senegal, which have developed considerably.

Now Tirera is a well-known celebrity in Senegal. The Senegalese media have nicknamed him "Made in China", and Tirera likes this title. "In China, I have realized my Chinese dream. My company has grown from small business to big exporter. While I continue to create wealth, I am also introducing Senegal to many Chinese people so that they can know more about my country. It is glorious to me that I help Chinese people learn more about my motherland, and to serve as a bridge of trade and friendship between China and Senegal."

Tirera says that Yiwu has earned a good reputation in Africa and the rest of the world, and he does his bit for this. He firmly believes that

as long as Yiwu continues to develop, his trading business will flourish. "It has been 40 years since China implemented its policy of reform and opening-up, and I have lived in China for 16 years. I'm one of the witnesses of this policy. As far as I'm concerned, my life underwent earth-shattering changes when I came to China. I have lived in China and experienced the implementation of the policy of reform and opening-up. I think that China wants to attract even more foreign business people."

Over the years, Tirera has witnessed many changes in Yiwu: the market has expanded, many skyscrapers have appeared, and English signs can be seen in hospitals, administrative service centers and other places, which helps those foreigners who can't speak Chinese handle matters smoothly. The investment and trade environment here is friendly. Tirera says that it is an open and inclusive city. The local government often organizes discussions with foreign business people to listen to their ideas, solicit their suggestions, heed their needs and help them solve problems.

"I have been living in China for nearly 20 years. I love China very much. I have realized my dream here, and I'm leading a good life with my own business. It is China that has given me this chance. I want to express thanks to China and its people."

— 义乌客商非洲来 —

塞内加尔商人苏拉来义乌经商16个年头了，早已经入乡随俗，养成了饮茶的习惯。“有朋自远方来，不亦乐乎。”如今的他喜欢以茶会客，现在他正坐在茶几边和朋友聊着天。在攀谈的过程中，苏拉的手也没有闲着，洗茶、冲泡、封壶等一系列茶道流程信手拈来，片刻间，一壶清香四溢的好茶已经摆在桌面上。苏拉说，他现在无论在哪儿都是茶不离手，和世界各地的朋友一道喝喝茶、聊聊天，可以拉近彼此的关系。中国人的生意经都蕴含在茶道之中，不疾不徐，礼尚往

来，好东西要大家分享。可见，他已深谙此道。

“喝一杯咖啡可能一两分钟就结束了，但是喝茶就不一样，它可以让朋友更久地留在我的办公室。朋友原本想说的可以说，原本可能没有目的性的谈话没准儿也能聊出新的合作构想，很多生意就是这么促成的，这是一件特别好的事情。”苏拉不仅中文讲得好，对于中国人的社交习惯也是非常了解的。

创业初期，苏拉从广州采购服装出口到塞内加尔，他从什么都不懂到熟练地砍价、发货，经历过很多困难，也得到过很多中国合作伙伴的帮助，淘到了人生中的第一桶金。两年后他又在朋友的介绍下来到了义乌，他发现这座城市真的是贸易行业的“宝藏”，万千商品琳琅满目，只有想不到的，没有买不到的。从此，苏拉开始改行主营五金产品的生意。义乌科瑞丝通外贸有限公司就是苏拉在中国的“总部”。经过这些年的发展，这家公司已经成为义乌最大的非洲商贸公司。

“物美价优的商品，高效便捷的服务，四通八达的物流，义乌的经商环境越来越好了。我们公司发展得也还算可以，2007 年

时公司只有一个员工，现在有40多个员工，业态持续发展，现在一年的营业额能达到4至5个亿，这是我十几年前想不到的事情。义乌良好的经济政策给予了外商很多帮助。同时在这里经营贸易的外商们也算是参与到义乌蓬勃发展的一份子，见证了这个城市的伟大和传奇。”苏拉略微有些得意地说。

一些非洲朋友得知苏拉的生意越做越大，便找上门来，希望他能带回更多品类的商品。现在，他除了自己经营的五金生意外，还要为来自非洲其他国家的客商采购餐具、饰品、日用百货、玩具等上千种小商品。“这些工业产品非洲都无法自己生产，要依赖进口。同亚洲的其他国家相比，中国义乌的产品可以凭借质量和价格的优势争取到这些订单，而且在非洲大家都非常认可这些‘中国制造’。”苏拉说。

其实中国文化和非洲文化有很多相似之处：中国人接待远道而来的客人时，会做一整桌子菜，哪怕客人根本吃不完；而在塞内加尔，主人会买一整只羊当面屠宰，用最新鲜的羊肉为客人制作美食。中国和塞内加尔都是热情好客的国家。现在也有很多中国企业被苏拉介绍到塞内加尔投资建厂，有着不错的规模和发展。

如今的苏拉早已是塞内加尔家喻户晓的名人。塞内加尔媒体称苏拉是“中国制造”，苏拉本人也喜欢这样的描述。“我在中国实现了自己的中国梦，从做小生意发展成今天这个规模，在不断创造价值的同时也在中国为塞内加尔做了宣传，让更多中国人来了解塞内加尔这个国家。在中国宣传自己的祖国，做中塞贸易和友谊的桥梁，对我来说也是十分光荣的事。”

苏拉说，“中国义乌”在非洲乃至全球的声誉不断提升，他也是其中的参与者。他坚信，义乌发展好了，自己的外贸生意肯定

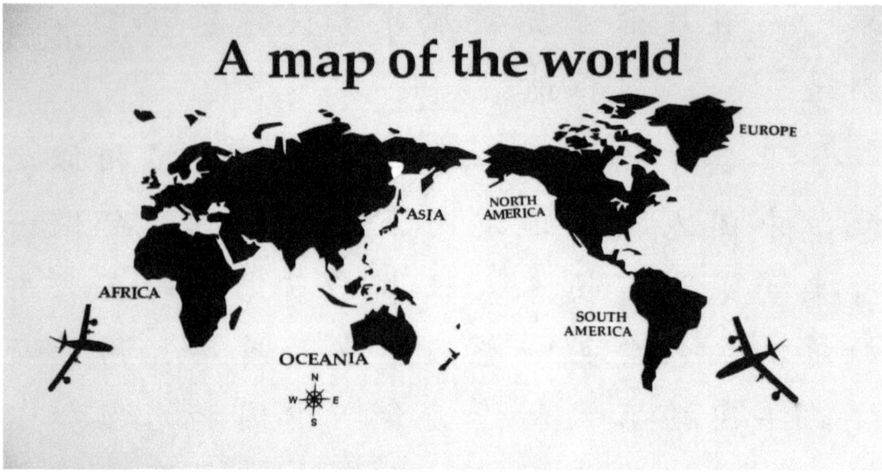

会更好。“中国改革开放40周年，我在中国生活了16年，也算是改革开放的见证者之一。就我自己而言，来中国之前和来中国以后，是完全不一样的感觉，我有着翻天覆地的变化。我体验到中国的生活，我体验到中国的改革开放，我体验到中国想多吸引更多的外国人来中国发展。”

这些年，苏拉亲眼见证了义乌方方面面的变化：市场变得越来越大，高楼大厦鳞次栉比，在医院、行政服务中心等地处处都有英文标识，即使是不会一句中文的外国人也能够顺利办事。这里的投资和贸易的环境真的是太友好了。苏拉说，义乌是一个开放又包容的城市，政府经常会组织外国商人举行

座谈，征询大家的想法和建议，考虑大家的需求，帮助大家解决问题。

“我在中国将近20年，我非常爱中国。我在中国实现了自己的梦想，有了今天的生活，有了今天的平台。是中国给了我这么一个平台，谢谢中国人民，也谢谢中国！”

Scan for a Video

出版策划：王君校　韩　晖
统筹协调：付　眉　韩　颖　彭　博
策划编辑：张　超
责任编辑：杨　晗
英文翻译：吴爱俊　薛彧威　卢　敏　范逊敏
英文编辑：卢　敏
封面设计：智玖拾（成都）文化传媒有限公司
排　　版：北京几何创想艺术设计有限公司
印刷监制：汪　洋

图书在版编目(CIP)数据

第三只眼看中国 . 我与中国共成长 : 汉、英 / 王新玲 , 杨丹主编 . -- 北京 : 华语教学出版社 , 2021.3

ISBN 978-7-5138-2082-0

Ⅰ . ①第… Ⅱ . ①王… ②杨… Ⅲ . ①新闻—作品集—中国—当代—汉、英 Ⅳ . ① I253

中国版本图书馆 CIP 数据核字 (2021) 第 035017 号

第三只眼看中国：我与中国共成长

王新玲 杨丹 主编

*

© 华语教学出版社有限责任公司

华语教学出版社有限责任公司出版
（中国北京百万庄大街 24 号　邮政编码 100037）
电话 : (86)10-68320585, 68997826
传真 : (86)10-68997826, 68326333
网址 ： www.sinolingua.com.cn
电子信箱 ： hyjx@sinolingua.com.cn
北京虎彩文化传播有限公司印刷
2021 年（16 开）第 1 版
2023 年第 1 版第 3 次印刷
（汉英）
ISBN 978-7-5138-2082-0
009800